MURDERED BY WORDS

A Midwest Cozy Mystery - Book 1

BY

DIANNE HARMAN

Published by: Dianne Harman
www.dianneharman.com

Interior, cover design and website by
Vivek Rajan Vivek
www.vivekrajanvivek.com

ISBN: 978-1530741250

CONTENTS

ACKNOWLEDGMENTS

First let me say, I am so grateful to have you as a reader. You're the reason my books have climbed to the top of the charts. Thank you, thank you, thank you! This book is the first in the Midwest Cozy Mystery Series. I hope you enjoy it as much as you've enjoyed the books in my other three cozy mystery series, Cedar Bay, Liz Lucas, and High Desert. I grew up in the Midwest, and while this book is fiction, and the characters don't exist in real life, I think there's a lot of the Midwest in it.

As always, I'm indebted to the two people I rely on to make my books so popular. First there is Vivek, who patiently formats my books for both print and digital, as well as designing wonderfully inventive book covers. I sent him an email that I was totally frustrated with what the cover of this book should look like, and within hours I received the beautiful cover that adorns this book. He has some sort of a sixth sense that seems to read my mind, and he's always able to create appropriate, and I think, beautiful covers. The second person is my best friend, my husband Tom. He's very careful to make sure that my books are as error free as possible, particularly as to time and characters. Thanks to both of you!

And as I usually do, I need to thank my dog, Kelly, (named after Kelly of Kelly's Koffee Shop, the first in the Cedar Bay Cozy Mystery Series), for becoming mature enough that I can now write while she amuses herself without getting into trouble. Thanks, Kelly!

Lastly, you may wonder why a Rottweiler and a West Highland Terrier play an important role in this book. Why those breeds? Truth be told, I don't have a clue! I've just always liked them, and as I wrote this book, I became enamored with Jazz and Rudy! I think you will be too.

Amazing Ebooks & Paperbacks for FREE

Go to www.dianneharman.com/freepaperback.html and get your FREE copies of Dianne's books and Dianne's favorite recipes immediately by signing up for her newsletter.

Once you've signed up for her newsletter you're eligible to win autographed paperbacks. One lucky winner is picked every week. Hurry before the offer ends.

PROLOGUE

It was a beautiful clear Midwest winter day in the small town of Lindsay, Kansas. Nancy didn't know it would be the last day of her life. She was planning on spending a few hours editing the final draft of Kat's latest book, The Country Club Cover-Up.

She was busily searching her office for the draft manuscript of the book when the doorbell rang. Looking at her watch, she thought Kat must have misunderstood what time she was supposed to come by the house or had decided to come early. She yelled down the hall, "Come in. The door's unlocked." She looked up from her desk and said "Oh, I was expecting someone else." They were the last words Nancy Jennings ever spoke.

CHAPTER ONE

Katherine Denham, who went by the name of Kat, made a mental list of what was on her agenda for the day. While she was thinking about what to do first, she idly petted Jazz, her West Highland Terrier. The fluffy dog looked up adoringly at her, his big black eyes a vivid contrast to the whiteness of his coat. Wherever Kat went, Jazz usually went too. She'd even gotten a large tote bag, so she could carry the dog with her when she ran errands. Jazz didn't like to stay home, so the tote bag was perfect for the little dog. She was glad Jazz was small for her breed and only weighed ten pounds.

She had an appointment at Susie's Salon at ten, and as she walked by the mirror hanging on the wall outside her office, she saw a few grey hairs starting to show. *Glad I'm going to get those taken care of today.*

Susie was a master at making Kat's dark blond hair look natural, but a few more days of growth, and Kat knew it would be very apparent to everyone she wasn't a natural blond but more of a bottle blond. She stopped and took a long look at herself in the mirror, wondering what others saw when they looked at her. The years had been kind to her face and body. Dark blue eyes looked back at her from a face which had its share of both laugh and life lines, but at fifty, she thought that was to be expected. Gravity had rearranged parts of her body a bit, but from the looks and smiles she got from men, she knew she still had a look that appealed to a number of them. The ringing of her cell phone pulled her out of her reverie.

"Hi, Lacie," she said to her daughter when she saw her name pop up on her cell phone screen. "How was the exam this morning?"

"Much easier than I thought it would be. Logic is just not my thing. With help from Austin and a couple of his fraternity brothers over at the Pi Kappa Alpha fraternity house I was able to get through it. The Pikes have a huge file drawer down in the basement of their house with copies of all the previous tests my logic professor has given for the past five years. It was a big help to see what his previous test questions were.

"Actually, I think I might have the best grades this semester I've had since I've been in college. Of course, almost anything would be better than the minimum C average I had the first semester I was here at the university. At least it allowed me to get initiated into the sorority. I didn't want to embarrass you by not having the grade average required for initiation, and I was pretty close to doing that."

"Honey, that's great news. I'm sure that will make your sorority happy. Still glad you pledged the Pi Beta Phi sorority?"

"Very much so. I've made a lot of good friends, but it does take up a lot of my time. I'm required to go to a lot of events, and there are also house meetings and all kinds of other stuff."

"Although I would have loved for you to have stayed home for a year or so and be a townie, I think it was a very good decision on your part when you opted to live in the sorority house. Jazz and I miss you, and the house still seems empty without you, but we're pretty much used to it by now."

"So how was the big golf dinner at the country club last night? Did you have fun with the new District Attorney? What do you have going on today?" Lacie asked.

"I have to go to Susie's for my regular hair appointment, then I'm meeting Bev at the country club for lunch. After that I have a meeting with Nancy to go over her edits of my latest book, and yes, I had a good time last night. I'll tell you all about it when I see you."

"Mom, I wish you'd give up writing the kinds of books you write. I know you said you make a lot of money writing them and believe me, I'm glad you're using a pen name so your true identity remains anonymous, but what if someone finds out you're the one who wrote them? After all, your books aren't exactly G-rated, they're more like X-rated."

Kat laughed and said, "It amazes me how many people buy them. When your father died he left me with the proceeds of a nice life insurance policy, but neither of us expected him to die at such a young age. I'm learning it takes quite a few dollars to maintain us in the manner to which we've become accustomed, and if my writing helps to put bread on the table, so be it. One of these days I'll write a book you can tell your friends about, but for now I'll stick with the steamy romance novels my fans have grown to expect from me."

"Mom, what would happen if people found out that the author of the books you write is a middle-aged woman living in a small Kansas college town who went to church almost every Sunday?"

"I have no idea, and I have no intention of finding out. Who would have thought women who live on farms or ranches could have such great sex with cowboys, military men who have just returned from overseas duty, or any other man who comes sniffing around, if you know what I mean?"

"Mom..."

"Gotta go, sweetheart, or I'll be late for my appointment with Susie, and you know how she feels about customers who are late."

"Tell me about it. Last time I got my hair cut I was late, and she really let me know about it! Have a good day, and I'll call you in a day or so."

"Thanks for calling, Lacie. I love you."

"Love you too, Mom."

CHAPTER TWO

Kat put Jazz in her tote bag and said a silent prayer to the gods who determined how much a dog was going to weigh. At ten pounds Jazz was small for her breed and looked like a stuffed animal toy. The only thing that told someone she was for real were her big intelligent saucer-like black eyes. She looked at Kat as they walked out the door as if to say, "Where to now?"

Ten minutes later, Kat pulled into the parking lot of Susie's Salon, popular with the local women who were always anxious to gossip and find out the latest rumor about what was happening in the small college town of Lindsay, Kansas. Kat loved the town with its old red brick buildings and houses. The tree-lined streets showcased many majestic old elm trees. When her husband, Greg, had been the head of the English Literature Department at the university, they'd lived a block away from the campus, so he could walk to work. After his untimely death in an auto accident, Kat and her daughter, Lacie, had moved to the other side of town. The house they'd shared with Greg held too many memories, and it was too painful to stay in the house. Greg's death had occurred over two years earlier, and Kat knew in her heart it was time to get out and make new friends. Lacie had encouraged her to accept the male invitations that had begun to come her way, but she'd been resistant.

She thought back to the party at the country club. She hadn't wanted to go to Nancy Jennings' holiday party, but several of her friends insisted she attend. They told her she was becoming a hermit, and that's the last thing Greg would have wanted her to be. Privately she wished she'd dropped out of the club after Greg had died, but even though Lacie was almost twenty-one, she still loved to play tennis and the club was known in that part of the state as having one of the best tennis programs for young people. Kat knew Lacie had benefited greatly from the time she'd spent in the program. Lacie was another one who felt she should attend the holiday party.

The club had been decorated for Christmas with several large pine trees that were displayed in the long hall that separated the pro shop from the dining room and bar. Brightly colored ornaments and white twinkling lights played against the green trees, each of which was surrounded by numerous large potted red poinsettias. Kat helped herself to some of the appetizers the club was known for and accepted a glass of wine from a waiter. She looked around and saw her editor, and now close friend, Nancy Jennings, waving for her to come join the group she was with. She walked over to the group and recognized several long-time members of the club.

Nancy's husband, Carl Jennings, stood next to Kat and when Nancy was deep in a conversation with a woman Kat didn't recognize, he turned to Kat and said, "I know Nancy is your editor, but I don't like her reading and editing the type of trash you write. That sex stuff is pretty sick," he angrily hissed. "Might give Nancy some ideas, and she might wonder if our sex life could be better. Just wanted to let you know I'm going to tell her you need to look for another editor, that, or I'll tell everyone I know that Sexy Cissy is really Katherine Denham." Kat looked back at him in shocked silence and couldn't think of anything to say in response to his veiled threat.

A moment later she realized their group had been joined by Blaine Evans, the man who had won the Seton County District Attorney's race a few weeks earlier. She recognized him from his campaign billboards and the political mail she'd received about him. Carl smiled at him, put his hand out to shake Blaine's and said, "Congratulations on your election victory, Blaine. I'm Carl Jennings, and a lot of us are very glad you won."

"Thanks, but I'd be less than honest if I didn't tell you I'm really glad the race is over." He turned to Kat and said, "I don't think I've had the pleasure of meeting you. I'm Blaine Evans."

Carl said, "This is Kat Denham. Her husband died tragically a couple of years ago, and this is the first time she's been to one of the club parties since then. It's good to have her back."

Kat couldn't believe the man smiling at her and saying those kind words was the same man who just a few minutes earlier had threatened to expose her if she didn't find a new editor. She'd met Carl and occasionally seen him after she and Nancy became friends, but tonight she was a seeing a side of him she'd never seen before. She and Blaine shook hands, and she was surprised to find she felt somewhat attracted to him, and she sensed the feeling seemed to be mutual. At the end of the evening, he asked if he could walk her to her car. When she'd gotten into her car, he surprised her by saying, "I'm the president of the Men's Club here at the country club, and every year at this time we have a dinner party and present awards. The event is tomorrow night, and I'd like to invite you to be my date. I know it's short notice, but I'd really be pleased if you would accept."

Everything Lacie and all of her friends had said about it being time caused her to say, "I'd very much like that. What time is it?"

"Cocktails are at 6:00. Why don't I pick you up at 5:30? I probably should be here a little early and make sure everything has been taken care of."

"Thank you, Blaine. I'll see you tomorrow night." She wrote down her address and handed it to him.

Wonder if Carl will tell him what kind of books I write. Oh well, no point in worrying about it. I'm not forcing anyone to read my books. If they enjoy them and it provides an income for Lacie and me, so be it. Anyway, I'd like to think my books are done in good taste!

CHAPTER THREE

Promptly at 5:30 in the evening on the following day, the doorbell at Kat's home rang. She opened the door and said to Blaine, "Welcome to my home. I hope you didn't have any trouble finding it. Please, come in."

"Kat, you look beautiful. I'm really glad you can go to the dinner at the country club with me. The people we'll be sitting with are pretty nice, and I think you'll enjoy the evening."

"I'd offer you a glass of wine, but you said you need to get to the club early to check on things. Does that still hold?" Kat asked.

"Yes, even though I'd love one, I think we better go. Since I'm the Men's Club president, it probably wouldn't look good if I arrived late and had alcohol on my breath. I'll take a rain check."

Kat got her purse, locked the door, and walked with him out to his car. As he opened the door for her, she made a mental note that he was a gentleman as well as being attractive. His hair was greying at the temples, and his tan face spoke of time spent outdoors pursuing his sport of choice, golf. He was almost a foot taller than Kat and surprisingly trim for being middle-aged, but what made him so attractive, in Kat's judgment, was his dazzling smile which lit up his entire face. She smiled back at him as she got in the car, looking forward to the evening ahead.

"Here we are," he said, pulling up to the valet stand at the country club. The valet opened Kat's car door as Blaine handed his car keys to him.

"Good to see you, Mr. Evans. You're here for the awards dinner, right? I'll have your car ready for you when it's over. I'll park it over there, so you won't have to wait."

"Thanks, Scott. I appreciate it. Ready, Kat?"

They started to walk up the steps when Kat noticed a book on the valet stand. It was one of hers called Montana Madness. "Scott, I hope we're not keeping you from your book," she said.

He blushed and said, "It's not mine. I mean, I wouldn't read that kind of a book, but my girlfriend read it and said it was really good. She told me it would really start my motor, if you know what I mean."

Blaine placed his hand on Kat's back and said, "We know what you mean, Scott." He turned to Kat and said, "I used to look at Playboy magazine when I was his age. I don't have kids, but I guess some things never change." Kat willed her face not to turn red and possibly prompt an inquiry from Blaine.

As soon as they entered the club a burly red-haired man walked over to Blaine. He introduced Kat to Mike Williams, the vice-president of the Men's Club. Mike shook her hand and started talking to Blaine.

"You're at the head table. When everyone's seated for dinner, just say a few welcoming words and tell them the program will begin during dessert. You'll introduce the annual club winners for the various categories and give them their trophies. When you're finished with that, you'll introduce Jason Wright, the winner of this year's PGA Master's Tournament. He's scheduled to speak for about twenty minutes. I've put a script up at the podium for you and made the print really large, so you shouldn't have a problem reading it. Don't tell me. I know, your eyesight isn't as good as it once was. Hey, at our age, is anything as good as it once was?" he asked, laughing as he left for the bar.

"May I get you a drink?" Blaine asked Kat.

"Yes, I'd like a glass of white wine. I don't know much about golf other than occasionally watching it on TV, but isn't getting the winner of the Master's Tournament to speak at the dinner a pretty big deal?"

"It's huge. Cost a bloody fortune to get him here, but the members were willing to ante up, so it's their call. That's probably why we have such a large turnout tonight."

The next hour went by in a haze, and Kat had to admit she was having a wonderful time. Although most of the women were her age, there were several who were definitely "trophy wives," but she didn't feel at all intimidated by them and was actually enjoying being in a social setting once again. Blaine couldn't have been more attentive. He was constantly introducing her and whispering in her ear who so-and-so was. Even though Kat knew a few of the people who were attending the banquet, most of the faces were new to her. Blaine had a good sense of humor and some of his asides caused her to laugh outright several times.

When it was time for dinner they found their table and sat down. A few minutes later Blaine excused himself and stepped up to the podium. After saying some words of welcome to the members and their guests, he rejoined their table just as dinner was being served. Kat didn't know the cost of the tickets for the evening, but based on what was being served and having the winner of the Masters speak at the dinner, she was pretty sure it had to be very hefty. That didn't even take into account the two bottles of expensive Napa wine, Cakebread cabernet sauvignon, that had been placed on each table.

The event was sponsored by the Men's Club, and dinner reflected it. From the wedge salad with bacon bits, crumbled Roquefort cheese, bleu cheese dressing, and croutons, to the filet mignon and roasted red potatoes, it was definitely a man's meal. It was all delicious, however the highlight was the dessert, a stunning chocolate soufflé topped with whipped cream and shaved chocolate.

When the waiters began serving dessert, Blaine excused himself again and walked up to the podium. "Please, continue eating. Once again I want to thank all of you for coming tonight. I'd like to introduce this year's winners in the various categories." He proceeded to name the winners and congratulated each one when they came up to the podium to accept their trophy.

When he had finished with the presentations, he said, "Now for the moment you've all been waiting for. This is something I never thought I would have a chance to do, introduce a winner of the world famous Masters Golf Tournament. I've watched this man's career for the last fifteen years, beginning when he was a high school student at Lindsay High School. He won every golf tournament for Lindsay for four years in a row and received a full golf scholarship to the University of Kansas. I know it's a rival of our university," he said over the chorus of friendly boos, "but you have to admit that they've done a good job with their golf program. Anyway, after graduation this young man spent the next seven years winning one tournament after another, but the Masters always eluded him until this year. Please join me in giving a warm welcome to this year's winner of the Masters Golf Tournament, Jason Wright."

The crowd gave Jason a standing ovation. Each man there secretly wished he was the one standing in front of the room and had been the winner of the Masters. Jason gave an upbeat rah-rah "If I did it, you can do it" type of speech that the audience loved. Thirty minutes later, he stepped down from the podium, smiling at the thunderous ovation he received.

Blaine returned to the podium. "That concludes this evening's program. The bar will remain open for another hour. You're welcome to stay. I wish I could, but I have to be in court early tomorrow morning."

When he got back to the table he said, "Kat, I hope you don't mind if we leave a little early, but I really do have an early court appearance tomorrow on an important case my office is prosecuting."

"That's fine with me," she said as she stood up. She turned to the couple on her left, "I really enjoyed talking with you. I hope to see you again sometime soon."

Blaine interjected, "You probably will, because I'm hoping you'll accompany me to our annual dinner dance in two weeks. The tennis club and the golf club have a joint dinner annually, and it's our biggest social event of the year here at the country club."

"Thank you. I'd love to," Kat said.

"Have you ever played golf?" he asked a few minutes later as they waited for Scott to bring Blaine's car.

"Never. My daughter's an avid tennis player here at the club, but somehow physical exercise has never been my thing, however I do enjoy watching those who have mastered any sport."

When they got to her home, he parked the car, got out, opened her door, and walked her up to the porch. She turned to him, "Blaine, as Carl mentioned, my husband was killed in an auto accident over two years ago. I've been reluctant to go to social events since his death, but I really enjoyed tonight. Thank you so much." She stood on her tiptoes and kissed him on the cheek. "Again, thank you."

"I'll call you later this week with the details about the dinner dance, but I'm hoping we can do something before then."

"I'd like that," she said, "and good luck tomorrow morning."

CHAPTER FOUR

"Morning Kat. If you're here it means six weeks have gone by since your last appointment, but it's always good to see you. Sit down and let's get started working on those nasty grey hairs that I can see are starting to peek through."

"Thanks, Susie," she said, putting her tote bag with Jazz in it next to the hairdresser's stand and sitting back in the chair. "I'll have the usual color and trim. I've finally found a hairdo I like, and one that I can maintain without spending hours on it. I'm glad you talked me into it."

"While I'm putting the color on I've got a question for you."

"Sure. What is it?" Kat asked.

"I've always thought it would be a fun thing to write a book about all the things people tell me. I just found out you're an author, and I was hoping you could tell me how you got started."

Kat stared in the mirror at Susie, not believing what she had just heard. "What makes you think I'm an author?" she asked, her heart thumping in her chest.

"Well, yesterday Sally Lonsdale was in here, and she was madder than a wet hen. Said the type of writing you did was just sheer filth, and you shouldn't get paid a red cent for it. Said she didn't see how you had the nerve to show up in church on Sundays. She told me she knew you were the author of a new book about to be published called The Country Club Cover-Up even if you did use the pen name Sexy Cissy."

"Why would Sally Lonsdale say those things? What's she talking about?" Kat asked in an innocent tone of voice.

"From what she told me she'd been given a copy of the manuscript by someone at the country club. This person told her there was a note from you to Nancy Jennings attached to the manuscript. Apparently the manuscript fell out of Nancy's tote bag when she was having lunch at the club, and someone there picked it up. She said this person gave a copy of it to her and another guest at the club. She said she'd looked the name Sexy Cissy up on Amazon and discovered there were eight other novels published by an author that writes books using the name Sexy Cissy."

"Did she say who the person was at the country club that picked up the manuscript?" Kat asked.

"No, just that someone had given her a copy of a manuscript called The Country Club Cover-Up. It was about some woman who belonged to a country club, had married an older man, and then had a bunch of affairs. You know how religious Sally is, anyway, she said she was going to talk to Nancy and make sure that book never got published. Said it was an affront to every Christian woman in the world. I guess there was something in the book about the woman going to church on the same day she and a man who worked at the country club had a little secret meeting, if you get my drift. I kinda thought it sounded good, so I asked her if I could read it."

"What did she say?"

"Sally said absolutely not. She was shocked I would even think about reading it. Then she said something I thought was a little strange."

"What did she say?"

"It really bothered me. Her exact words were 'Sometimes people have to take things into their own hands, and I'm going to make sure that book never sees the light of day.' That was it. I don't know what she meant by it, but something about that book really got under her skin. Anyway, are you the author?"

"I know the person who is the author," Kat said, hoping that would take care of the question. She wasn't quite ready to assume the responsibility for being the person who wrote under the pen name of Sexy Cissy. Kat wasn't sure the small college town where she lived was ready for that kind of information.

"Okay, I can see you're not going to give me a straight answer. Actually, if I were you, I'd claim the name. A lot of my customers read books that have sex scenes in them. I could probably sell a lot of them for you. As a matter of fact, I'd like to carry them and sell them right here in the salon."

"Thanks. I'll keep it in mind. Oh, one other question. Do you know if Sally ever talked to Nancy?"

"I don't know. She mentioned she was going to go over to her house during the day while Carl was at work. She said she didn't mind being responsible for a book not getting published, but she drew the line at being responsible for Carl finding out that his wife was editing a smut book. She said Carl often spoke in church about how all the problems with the young people today were caused by the filth that was in movies and on television. She said she was sure he'd leave Nancy if he knew she was editing a book like that."

I wouldn't call The Country Club Cover-Up a smut book. Yeah, it's got some pretty sexy scenes in it, but the language is all G-rated. And who's to say there haven't been lots of women who have belonged to a country club and had an affair with one of the employees?

"Susie, you could do me a favor by not telling anyone about our conversation or your conversation with Sally. I'm not sure what I'm going to do about what she told you. I'd like you to keep it to yourself for now, if you wouldn't mind."

"Not a problem, Kat. You're a good customer, but I'm telling you, if that book ever sees the light of day, I'll be the first one in line to buy it. Matter of fact, think I'll go on Amazon and pick up a couple of other books Sexy Cissy has written, and no, you don't need to thank me," she said winking conspiratorially.

*****

"Jazz, I'm going over to the country club, but before I do I need to drop you off at home," Kat said as she took Jazz out of her tote and put her in the back seat. "The club has a strict policy that no animals are allowed on the premises unless it's a service dog, and having a Westie for a service dog would be a bit of a stretch I'm not willing to defend."

Kat pulled into her driveway, picked up Jazz, and as she entered the house through the kitchen door she heard the house phone ringing. Although Kat had a cell phone, about the only person who used it was Lacie. Most of the residents of Lindsay still preferred to use their house phones. She put the receiver up to her ear and said, "Hello. This is Kat. Hold on for a second while I put my dog down." She put Jazz on the floor and pushed the screen door open with her foot, so Jazz could go out in the yard.

"Thanks for holding. How can I help you?"

"Kat, this is Tiffany Conners," she said in an icy voice. "Do you know who I am?"

"Of course. We've met several times at the country club. Why do you ask?"

"Well, I just read a copy of the manuscript of some new book you're writing, the one Nancy Jennings is editing for you, and I was shocked to see what you wrote about me. I can't believe you're writing smut like that under the name of Sexy Cissy. It's disgusting.

You can't publish that filth."

"Wait a minute, Tiffany. I don't know what you're talking about," Kat said, hoping Tiffany couldn't hear her heart racing. She wondered if having her heart pound that hard twice in the space of a couple of hours was a healthy thing, and then she resumed listening to Tiffany.

"Oh, yes you do. You wrote that I'm having an affair. Do you know what will happen to my reputation and my marriage if my husband reads that? He'll divorce me, and I'll probably get kicked out of the Junior League. I know the only reason I ever got into that exclusive women's organization was because I'm married to Lester. I can't let that happen. You and Nancy are really sick people and quite frankly, don't deserve to live. The world has enough of your kind spreading filth and lies, so maybe it's time some of us took the steps necessary to get rid of them," she said as she slammed the phone down.

Good grief. How did she get a copy of my manuscript? I guess the good news is that she won't tell anyone about it, since she thinks the main character in the book, Chastity, is her. I suppose the only reason she must think that is because she actually is having an affair. Hmm. Wonder who it's with. Well, there's no way I'm not going to publish that book. It may have a little more sex in it than a lot of the residents of the little town of Lindsay, Kansas, would own up to, but based on the fact that Scott's girlfriend was reading one of my books, rather imagine there are a bunch of other people in this town who are too. What was it Shakespeare said in one of his plays? "I thinketh thou protesteth too much." Think that's what just happened with Tiffany.

CHAPTER FIVE

Even though Kat had attended Nancy's party and been to the awards dinner with Blaine, it had been a long time since she'd had lunch at the country club restaurant, and she wondered if the gossipy daytime dining room hostess Barbara was still there. She got her answer when she saw Barbara standing at the hostess desk. "Hi, Barbara. I'm meeting Bev Simpson. Is she here yet?"

"No, she's not, Mrs. Denham. It's good to see you again. Would you like to be seated or wait for her?"

"I think I'd like to be seated now. When she gets here, please send her to my table."

"Sure. Follow me." When Kat was seated Barbara handed her a menu and then looked around to see if anyone was listening. She bent her head down and said, "This is the same table where Nancy Jennings sat a few days ago. I probably shouldn't say anything, but I found your manuscript after she left," she said giggling. "Wow, didn't know you were Sexy Cissy. Love what you write, but don't tell anyone I read that stuff."

"What makes you think I'm Sexy Cissy?" Kat asked, looking up at her.

"You wrote a note to Nancy and attached it to the manuscript. It was signed Kat. There aren't too many people in Lindsay who go by the name of Kat, plus I know you're a friend of Nancy's. Your name was on the guest list for the party Nancy recently had. I just put two and two together and figured out you had to be Sexy Cissy."

"Where is the manuscript? Did you give it back to Nancy?"

Barbara turned red and stuttered, "Uh, not exactly. Sally Lonsdale was sitting at the table next to where Nancy had been and saw me pick the manuscript up from under the table. She asked me what it was. I walked over to where she was sitting, and we both looked at it. The title 'The Country Club Cover-Up' was on the top of the manuscript. We both noticed a note with your name on it attached to the front page. Sally was interested, because she figured it was probably about our country club, and she asked me if I would make a copy of it for her. I didn't see any harm in doing that, since it was probably going to be published pretty soon anyway. I took it back to the office, made a copy, and gave it to her.

"After the lunch crowd left, I took my afternoon break and read the first couple of chapters of the manuscript. I figured out right away that the character in the book named Chastity was probably Tiffany Conners, or at least I was pretty sure it was her. After my break was over and I went back to work, I had to go into the bar area to get a drink for one of the customers. Tiffany was there, and I told her about the book. I didn't tell her I thought the main character was her. Anyway, she asked if she could have a copy of the book, so I made one and gave it to her.

"I was glad she wanted a copy. She always acts so snooty and everything. Treats me and everyone else on the staff like dirt. Have to tell you it made me feel really good knowing she'd be squirming like a worm on a fish hook when she read it. I know that's small of me, but like I said, it made me feel good."

So that's how Tiffany and Sally got the manuscript, Kat thought.

"Barbara, did anyone else see that manuscript?" she asked.

"I'd love to stay and talk, Mrs. Denham, but some people just walked in. I need to get back to the hostess desk," Barbara said as she abruptly ended the conversation and hurried away.

Kat took her phone out of her purse and called Nancy's cell phone. There was no answer. In the past she'd never called Nancy's house phone, because she hadn't wanted Carl to know about their relationship even though it was apparent he did based on what he'd said to her the other night. When Nancy's voice came on the line asking the caller to leave a message, she said, "This is Kat. I'm still planning on being at your house at 3:00 for our meeting. I hope you have the manuscript, because I just found out that Barbara at the club gave a copy of it to Tiffany Conners. I sincerely hope no one else has it. See you in a couple of hours."

After she ended the call Kat looked at the menu and saw that a number of new dishes had been added since she'd last visited the restaurant. Lacie had told her the club had hired a new chef and from the looks of the menu items, Kat decided he must have had some experience preparing food outside of Kansas. She wondered if he'd been responsible for the awards dinner at the club which she'd thought was delicious. Looking at the menu, it seemed that most of the dishes were basically Midwestern, but from the entrees she saw waiters carrying to tables, the chef was putting his own touch on them.

She was so deeply engrossed in the menu she didn't see Bev come in. She felt a tap on her shoulder and heard Bev say, "That new menu makes for good reading, but from what I'm hearing, what you write is even better." She took a seat across the table from Kat.

"It's been a long time since I've been here, and I can see that the new chef has made a lot of changes to the menu. It looks great, but wait, what were you saying about me writing?"

"Tell you in a minute. If you're ready to order I already know what I want. I probably should experiment, but I think the chef does something magical with the seafood salad. It has all the crab and shrimp in it that you'd ever want rather than the piddly two pieces of each that the other restaurants seem to always put on their salads. What sounds good to you?"

"I've got to try his version of meatloaf. I know it's a common dish, but from what I saw being served at the table next to us, it looks like the chef has taken it to a new level. I mean, who thinks to serve a brown gravy over meatloaf on spinach with swirled mashed potatoes on top of it and garnished with asparagus tips? Definitely can't get past that." They gave their orders to the waiter who filled their glasses with Perrier water.

"Kat, I'm so glad you're back among the living. First of all, you attended the golf dinner last night with our handsome new district attorney. Second of all, you're meeting me here for lunch. We haven't done this for way too long. Thirdly, even though I consider you one of my closest friends, I didn't know you were Sexy Cissy and wrote steamy hot novels."

Kat was biting into a carrot from the relish plate the waiter had brought. She stopped halfway through the bite and said, "What are you talking about? Who told you such things?"

"I'd say a little birdie, but I know you wouldn't believe me, so I'll be honest. I'll get to it in a minute. You know what a golf nut Jim is, and there is no way he'd turn down a chance to meet the winner of the Master's. We were at the dinner last night on the other side of the room from you. From what I could see, it looked like you and Blaine were thoroughly enjoying each other. Would that be correct?"

"I can't speak for him, but yes, I had a wonderful time. I think he must have enjoyed it too, because he asked me to go with him to the joint tennis and golf dinner dance weekend after next. I know he's the new district attorney, but I really don't know much about him. I thought I knew pretty much everyone in town and what with someone who's that much in the public eye, I'm surprised I've never met him before."

"I've known him for a long time. As a matter of fact, I thought of introducing you to him, but you were adamant you weren't ready to meet anyone. Let's see. He's fifty-two. He a scratch golfer and plays all the time with Jim. That's how I know him so well. He often plays nine holes in the morning before he goes to work, weather permitting."

She continued. "He's never been married. He was going to get married years ago, but a terrible tragedy intervened. When he was in his early thirties he fell in love with a woman from western Kansas. Her family farmed wheat, was very wealthy, and they had their own private plane. A week before she and Blaine were to be married she was flying to Kansas City for the final fitting of her wedding dress. Her father was flying the plane, and there was some malfunction with the gas in the plane. It exploded, and she and her father were both killed in the explosion. I didn't know Blaine then. He was living in Kansas City at that time. After the plane crash he moved to Lindsay and joined a friend from law school in his law practice."

"That's so sad. Poor man," Kat said.

"Yes. Jim told me he buried himself in his work for years, and the only two things he liked to do were play golf and involve himself in local Republican politics. That's one of the reasons he won the election. He's built up quite a large political network that helped him. Guess it was kind of payback time for all of the elections he'd worked on over the years, plus he's got a reputation for being a large donor to people who are running for office the first time."

"That certainly explains why I never met him. I don't know much about politics. It never interested me, but I suppose if I'm going to see him again, I probably should get up to speed on what's happening in the local political arena."

"Yes, you definitely should. By the way, Jim thinks the world of him, and so do I. I already told you how glad I am you've decided to join the land of the living again, but what I really want to get to is the third thing I mentioned, Sexy Cissy. When did you start writing those books? By the way, I looked Sexy Cissy up on Amazon and there's no photograph, so I was sure you were using a pen name. Actually, I bought a couple of the books on Kindle, and I'm about half-way through my first one. It's well-written, although I don't think I'd want my daughter to read it. From what I've read so far, there's a side to you I've obviously never seen," she said laughing.

"Bev, what makes you think it's me, and where did you hear it?"

"I was in Susie's Salon yesterday, and I overheard a conversation Susie was having with Sally Lonsdale about you, your book, and your editor, Nancy. I pretended I was reading an article in one of the magazines, but truth be told, I eavesdropped on every word. Sally was pretty worked up about it. Once I heard her talking about chastity belts, and how every young woman should have to wear one until they were married. I thought she was kidding, but she wasn't. She's always talking about how certain books should be banned from being on the shelf at the library. I mean she thinks Gone With The Wind is the work of the devil. She sounded angry enough to do away with you, your book, and your editor."

Kat shivered. "I don't think I've ever had someone be that angry with me. I don't like it. I've met her several times, but she wasn't someone I wanted much to do with. She seems pretty unbalanced to me.

"I believe that would be a perfect description of her. I see the waiter bringing our orders now. While we're eating, I want to hear all about your literary career, and I'm sure Sally would say that was the wrong term to use when referring to your books."

Kat took several bites of her meatloaf and said, "This is one of the best things I've ever had. You know how I love to cook, and if I ever have Blaine over for dinner, I'd love to experiment with this dish and serve it to him. Seems like a lot of work for just me eating alone."

"I didn't ask you about your food, I asked you about your literary career. Shoot."

Kat put her fork down and said, "Well, I guess I might as well tell you about it. I was hoping it wouldn't become public for a number of reasons, and from what I've heard today, I think I was right. After

Greg died, I didn't know what to do with myself. I'd been a reader, and like you, my major in college was English Literature. As you know, Greg and I met in college in an English class. After he went on to become the head of the English Literature Department at the university, our life pretty much consisted of being around writers and want-to-be writers."

"You still haven't told me how you started writing steamy page turners."

"One night I was surfing on the web and an ad popped up about how you could get rich by becoming an author. I clicked on it, and it had a bunch of charts about which types of books made the most money. Of course, the site it was on just happened to have courses you could take to write books on about every subject under the sun. What caught my eye was that some of the highest paid authors were those who wrote the steamy page turners, as you call them. I would prefer the term 'romance,' but my books probably are a little sexier than some of the romance novels.

"I knew at some point I was going to have to get a job, and I was really worried about my finances. You know I've never worked outside the home, and I figured the only thing available for a fifty-year-old woman with no work history would be an entry level job. I just couldn't see myself asking someone if they wanted fries with their hamburger, like that song Tim McGraw sang, but I wasn't sure I had any other options."

"Okay, you've told me where you got the idea. How did you start? Was it hard to come up with characters and a plot?"

"Not really. I've always had a pretty good imagination. After I read the Internet article I kept thinking that maybe I should give it a try. The rest is pretty much history. I wrote a book and happened to meet Nancy, my editor, about that time. She told me about the man she worked with who could design a cover for the book and format it as an e-book. After that, I put it up for sale on Amazon. The person who did the cover and formatting for me told me I needed to have a social media presence, so I became active on Twitter and Facebook under the name of Sexy Cissy. My books have done phenomenally well, and I'm making a lot of money from them. I'm really having fun with it, because I never considered myself to be very creative, but now my mind is always thinking of new ideas for books."

"I think it's great, and other than a few do-gooders, I imagine everyone else will too. You're really not doing anything all that different from what a lot of other authors do. They just haven't put their books in a series like you have, plus I imagine a few of the people who may criticize you have had fantasies like the ones you're writing about. How does Lacie feel about it?"

"She's still at an age where she's very concerned about what other people think. She'd rather no one found out, but it looks like it's too late for that. I will say it's helping to keep her in nice clothes and paying for her college education, to say nothing of the costs of the sorority. I could have afforded for her to go to college, but I think she would have had to live at home all four years rather than in the sorority house, and I certainly couldn't have afforded the nice car she drives. I hope she'll understand that when members of the community, including her friends, find out that I'm Sexy Cissy."

"I'm not sure I'd say it quite that way. I think saying that you write under the pen name of Sexy Cissy would be a better idea. I'm curious what Blaine's going to say. If it was Jim, he'd be thrilled if I wrote books like that. He'd probably be wondering where I got the ideas, and it sure couldn't hurt the physical part of our relationship."

"I've never even thought about telling Blaine. I don't feel like I know him well enough to tell him, but I don't want him to find out from someone else."

"Why don't you sit with it for couple of days? You don't need to make that decision right now." Bev looked at her watch. "I've got to go. Reba leaves at 3:00, and I need to pay her for cleaning the house." She motioned for the waiter to bring them the check. They each put their membership number on the check and signed it. "Talk to you later," Bev said, blowing a kiss to Kat as she walked away from the table.

CHAPTER SIX

Kat left the country club parking lot and decided she had just enough time to stop by her house and pick up Jazz on her way to Nancy's home.

I really hope Nancy's finished editing The Country Club Cover-Up. I want to read it once more and send it to Dirk, so he can format it. Once that's done, I'll publish it on Amazon and off it goes. I better clear my schedule for next week, so I can do some marketing and make sure everyone knows that my latest book in the Lusty Women Series has been published. My fans are going to love this one! I mean, what's not to love about Jake, the handsome ex-Green Beret who works at the country club where Chastity and her husband are members. Her husband hires him to fix some fences at their ranch, and he and Chastity end up having a steamy affair.

She parked on the street in front of Nancy's two-story brick house, its green shrubbery contrasting nicely with the brick's red tone. Nancy had decorated it for Christmas with twinkling lights outlining the windows, a huge wreath with a bright red bow on the front door, and a life-size manger scene on the front lawn. It was warm and inviting, just like Nancy's personality.

Kat thought back to the first time she'd met Nancy Jennings. It had been at a mother-daughter pledge class tea at the Pi Beta Phi sorority house during Lacie's first semester in college. They'd both been standing next to the table where an assortment of cookies was spread out. Nancy had leaned over to get a cookie when one of the other mothers accidentally jostled her arm, causing the contents of Nancy's tote bag to fall to the floor. Kat bent down to help Nancy pick up her things and saw a book with a lot of colored sticky notes attached to many of the pages. She remembered asking Nancy why she'd made so many notations in the book. Nancy had responded that she was an editor who worked out of her home editing books for various different authors. Kat asked if she was taking any new clients, and Nancy had said she was always willing to talk to someone about their work. She gave Kat her business card and asked her to call.

A few days later Kat called Nancy, and they had a long talk about Kat's book project. Kat explained to her that she had written her first book, but she wasn't sure what to do with it. When Nancy had asked her what genre she wrote in, Kat had hemmed and hawed. She could still remember how hot her cheeks had become when she told Nancy it was a book about a woman who had a steamy affair with a man who was doing some work at her ranch in Montana. Nancy had been quiet for a long time and then told her that although she'd never edited any books in that genre, she'd be happy to read it and give Kat her opinion of it.

Nancy had loved the book. They'd come to an agreement that no one would be told that Kat was the author. It was Nancy who had suggested the name for the series, Lusty Women, as well as Kat's pen name, Sexy Cissy. She'd also suggested that Kat hire Dirk, the formatter and cover designer Nancy worked with. He lived in India, and although Kat was sure she'd never meet him, his work was excellent, and his price was fair. Kat discovered early on that her fans were hungry for her books, and she needed to feed them a new book as often as possible. They, in turn, responded by making her one of the best-selling authors on Amazon.

It had been a mutually advantageous arrangement. The one thing Nancy had made her promise was that Kat would never tell Carl, her husband, about the Lusty Women Series. According to Nancy, Carl didn't pay much attention to the books she edited, so she didn't expect there would be any problems. She'd told Kat her husband was

---

quite straight-laced and would be shocked and angry to learn she was editing a book that drew a pretty fine line between erotica and romance. Kat had promised her that the only person who would know was Lacie, her daughter, and Lacie didn't want anyone to find out. She was certain the sorority would take a very dim view of having the mother of one of their members writing books like those in the Lusty Women Series.

As Kat walked up the steps to the front door of Nancy's house, she hoped that having to admit to people she wrote under the pen name of Sexy Cissy, and that she was the author of the Lusty Women Series, wouldn't be a problem for Nancy. Evidently Carl already knew based on the threatening remarks he'd made to Kat at the country club. She just hoped Nancy could convince him she was unaffected by what she edited, and she couldn't be a censor for what other people read. Kat thought maybe she'd have to tell Carl that freedom of speech was part of the Constitution, and it covered not only the spoken word but also words written on paper.

She knocked on the door and rang the doorbell. There was no answer. Later, Kat would look back on that moment as the last guilt-free moment of her life.

CHAPTER SEVEN

When Nancy hadn't come to the door after several minutes, Kat looked at her watch to make sure she had the right time. It showed it was straight up three in the afternoon, the exact time they were supposed to meet. One of the things that made Nancy such a good editor was her attention to detail. If she told Kat she was going to call her at a certain time, the phone always rang on the given minute.

Not being home at the agreed upon time was totally unlike Nancy. Kat hadn't talked to her since they'd made the appointment a few days earlier, and she wondered if Nancy was sick. She tried the door, and it easily opened. Jazz walked into the house a few steps in front of Kat. "Nancy," she called out, "anyone home?" No one answered. Kat had been to Nancy's home many times, and they'd always met in Nancy's office. *Maybe she's in her office and is so totally caught up in editing and concentrating so hard she didn't hear me,* Kat thought.

"Nancy, it's Kat. Are you here?" Again, there was no response, only total silence. She walked down the hall towards the office with Jazz at her side. As they entered the office, Jazz began barking furiously which was completely unusual for her.

"Jazz, no! Stop barking." The bark became a low whine and she sat down. "Jazz, come here," Kat said, but Jazz stayed where she was as if rooted to the spot. Kat walked over to where Jazz was sitting, and she saw Nancy sprawled on the floor in front of a bookcase with what looked like a bullet hole in her chest and blood pooled around her body. Kat stood there for several seconds, refusing to believe what her eyes were seeing.

Jazz whined again, startling Kat out of her reverie and forcing her to react to the scene in front of her. "Jazz, come," she screamed as she ran out of the house and got in her car, trying to put the vision of Nancy out of her mind. She panicked, not knowing what to do next. After a moment she reached in her purse to get her phone and call 911. When she opened it she saw Blaine's business card. Without thinking, she pressed in his numbers on her phone. Her call was answered immediately by him. "Hi Kat, I'm glad you called. I was going to call you later."

"Blaine, she's de, de, dead," Kat stuttered, her voice shaking with emotion.

"What are you talking about? Who's dead?"

"Nancy, my editor, she's dead. She has what looks like a bullet hole in her chest, and there's blood all around her body."

"Where are you, Kat? Can you give me an address? Is anyone with you?"

"I'm in my car in front of Nancy Jennings' house. The address is 175 Elm Lane. I'm by myself. No, Jazz, my dog, is with me."

"Oh no, not Nancy! She's the one who invited me to her holiday party where you and I met. I am so sorry, anyway, stay where you are. Lock the doors on your car. I'll get over there as fast as I can. I should be there in just a few minutes. If you feel faint, put your head between your legs. Don't talk to anyone or do anything until I get there. Promise?"

"Yes, please hurry," she whispered. When Blaine pulled up several minutes later, she was sitting behind the steering wheel of her car, sobbing uncontrollably.

"Have you called 911 or anyone else?" Blaine asked urgently when she opened her car door.

"No," she said, gulping. "For some reason the card you gave me last night was next to the phone in my purse, and for whatever reason I called you."

"I'm glad you did. I need to call Frank Michaelson, the chief of police. Sorry, Kat, but he's going to want to talk to you and so will a few of his men. Does her husband know?"

"No one knows, except the person who did this. Carl and their daughter need to be told. Her daughter's in the same sorority as my daughter, Lacie. What should I do?"

"Nothing for the moment. Nancy's name won't be publicly released until the next of kin are notified. I'll tell Frank, and he can decide what he wants to do. Just stay where you are. I'll call him now," Blaine said, stepping away from her car.

Kat sat in her car and absent-mindedly stroked Jazz who was shivering and shaking. At some level the little dog seemed to know something terribly wrong had happened. She finally stopped whining and settled down. Kat saw Blaine talking into his phone and shortly after he had finished the call she saw the flashing red and blue lights of a police car. It was almost immediately joined by three other police cars.

A large man got out of one of the cars and walked over to Blaine, who gestured to the car where Kat was sitting. Blaine motioned for her to join them. She got out of her car and left Jazz in it. She was a little unsteady on her feet and Blaine gently held her elbow. The big chief of police looked at Kat and said, "Kat, I remember you from when we had a class in school together. I didn't associate the last name of Denham with you. I knew you by your maiden name of Liggins. Sorry, my mistake."

"No problem. I'm not thinking very clearly at the moment, anyway."

"Kat, I want to take a statement from you, but first I need to go in the house. Where did you find Mrs. Jennings?"

"She's in her office. There's blood all around her, and it looks like she has a gunshot wound in her chest." Kat put her head in her hands and started sobbing again. "Why would anyone want to kill Nancy? It doesn't make any sense to me."

"Stay here, and I'll be back in a few minutes." He gestured to the three policemen who were standing by their cars waiting for the chief's instructions. They followed him into the house. The chief returned a few minutes later and said, "I'm sorry, Kat, but I do need to talk to you. Can you go into the house, or do you want to talk to me out here?"

"I really don't want to go back in there. Could we sit in the chairs on the porch instead?"

"Yes. While I was in the house I called a couple of people from my office to come and dust the house for fingerprints. We'll need to get yours as well. It's just a formality." Frank, Blaine, and Kat sat down on the padded porch chairs. Frank was the first to speak. "I'd like you to tell me why you were here and what you saw."

"I was supposed to meet Nancy here at her house at 3:00 this afternoon. I knocked and rang the doorbell, but no one answered. The door was unlocked, so I let myself in. I kept calling out, but there was no response. I thought maybe she was concentrating so hard on whatever it was she was doing that she didn't hear me. I walked down the hall and went into her office. My dog started barking, and that's when I saw her." She again covered her face with her hands and began sobbing.

"Kat, why were you meeting Nancy today?"

She was quiet for several moments and then she began to speak in a soft voice. "I'm an author, and Nancy was my editor. We were going to discuss my latest book." She avoided looking at Blaine.

"Kat, you never told me you were an author. When you called me a few minutes ago, you said your editor was dead. I couldn't figure out what you meant," Blaine said. "I'm surprised you didn't say anything last night."

She looked from Blaine to Frank and then back at Blaine, knowing that what she was going to say in the next few minutes might be the kiss of death for having any type of a relationship with him. "I don't write under my name. I use the pen name Sexy Cissy," she said quickly. "Nancy was my editor, but she didn't want her husband to know, so you won't see any of my books in her bookcase."

"You're Sexy Cissy?" the police chief asked incredulously. "I can't believe it. My wife's a huge fan of yours. Think it's one of the reasons our marriage has had a second start. She loves your books."

"Guess I'm the one in the dark, here," Blaine said. "Obviously I don't know anything about this, but I'd be very curious to have you tell me how you started writing books with that pen name, Kat."

"I will, but I don't think my books are relevant to Nancy being murdered."

Just then a car raced into the driveway, a man flung the door open, and ran up the steps. "Chief, one of your men just came to my office and told me Nancy has been murdered. Is that true? Where is she? I can't believe this," Carl blurted out with a stricken look on his face.

Frank walked over to him and put his large hand on Carl's shoulder. "I'm sorry you found out that way, Mr. Jennings. I try to make it my practice to personally tell the decedent's family when someone has died, but since this is a murder case, I had to stay here and make sure everything is being done properly, so we can find out who did this. Your wife is in her office. I'll go in with you."

After they left, Kat looked at Blaine and said, "If you want to cancel our date for the dinner dance, I'd understand."

33

"Why would I want to do that?" he asked.

"Well, word is bound to get out that I'm Sexy Cissy. As a matter of fact, from what I heard today it's already out. Anyway, I don't want to embarrass you."

"Kat, I'm fifty-two years old. I rather think there's not much in your books that will shock or surprise me. This isn't the time or the place, but if we do develop some type of a relationship, and I'd like to, it might make it interesting. Don't worry about me."

He stopped talking as they heard sounds of shouting coming from inside the house. "She's responsible for my Nancy being murdered. Nancy should have never edited the filth that woman writes. Mark my words, she did it, or she knows who did it. She probably killed Nancy when Nancy told her she wouldn't be her editor anymore because of the smut she writes. I demand you arrest her for murder."

The door burst open and Carl strode out of the house and pointed a finger at Kat, tears streaming down his face. "I know you're responsible for Nancy's murder. I told you to leave her alone, but you didn't, did you? Did you shoot her when Nancy told you she was through working for you? She was too good for you. Mark my words, I'll make sure what happened to Nancy happens to you."

"Carl, those are pretty harsh words. Don't think we need any threats being made after what's happened here. Is there someone I can call for you?" the chief asked.

"Yes, you can call my brother, Doug Jennings. His phone number is on the refrigerator. He's retired and only lives a few blocks from here."

"Wayne," Frank said to the policeman who had followed Carl out of the house, ready to restrain him if it was necessary, "call his brother and ask him if he can come over here right now. Tell him there's been a family emergency."

Carl stared angrily at Kat for several moments and then went back in the house. Blaine and Kat heard Carl tell the chief that when his brother got there the two of them would go over to the sorority house and tell Carl's daughter, Nicole.

Blaine turned to Kat and said, "Let me check with Frank and see if it's okay for you to leave. Why don't I follow you home? Are you sure you can drive, or would you like me to drive you home?"

"I'm okay, but I really do want to get home."

He returned a few minutes later. "Frank said you're free to go, and he'll call you if he needs any more information from you. He asked that you call him if you think of something else."

CHAPTER EIGHT

Kat opened the front door of her house and let Jazz in. "Please come in, Blaine. I'm really torn about a few things, and I'd like to talk to you about them if you don't mind. Have a seat, and I'll be back in just a minute. I need to let Jazz outside."

"No problem. I need to call my office and tell them I won't be back for the rest of the day. It's already five-fifteen, so they've probably figured that out and may have left for the day."

When she returned, he said, "You've had a grueling couple of hours. May I get you a drink or a glass of wine?"

"Thanks," she said as she sat down on the plaid couch in the family room which was attached to the kitchen. "There's an open bottle of white wine in the refrigerator, and I'd love a glass. If you'd like something stronger, look in the cabinet above the refrigerator. There's mix in the frig."

A few moments later he handed her a glass of wine and took a sip of the drink he'd made for himself. "Kat, there's something you need to know. I received an anonymous call at my office today from someone who told me they thought I should know that you and Sexy Cissy are the same person. I didn't pay any attention to it at the time, but now I wonder if it had something to do with Nancy's murder. Why don't you start at the beginning and tell me how this whole thing came about?"

For the next hour Kat told him about writing her first book out of fear that the insurance money her husband had left her would run out, how she'd met Nancy at the sorority house, and how popular the books she wrote had become.

"I've never read one of your books, so I think I'll probably go on Amazon tonight and get one," ...

She interrupted him by saying, "I'll be back in a minute." She returned with a paperback in her hand. "Take this. It's my latest book. I'd autograph it for you, but given the circumstances, that doesn't sound very appropriate." She handed the book to him.

He looked at it and then over at her. "Nice cover of a cowboy and a beautiful woman. Is that your trademark?"

"Kind of, and I have no idea why I started writing about ranches, farmers, and cowboys. It just seemed to work. I write a series called the Lusty Women Series, and all of the books in it deal with women who live on ranches and the cowboys or farm workers that develop relationships with them. The one Nancy was editing was a little different in that although the woman lived in town, her husband was a banker, and they owned a ranch. She was having an affair with a ranch hand who also worked at the local country club. I guess they've struck a chord somewhere, because the sales of my books have pleasantly surprised me. I was worried I'd be flipping hamburgers in some fast food restaurant by now, but the book sales have definitely kept the wolf away from my door."

"I'm glad for you, but I'm a prosecutor, and there are some things that are beginning to make me nervous. First of all, I get a phone call at my office about you, and secondly, the decedent's husband accuses you of murder. Is there anything you can tell me about the reaction of readers to your books?"

She began by telling him about Susie, her hairdresser, and what she had told Kat about the woman named Sally Lonsdale, who was greatly opposed to the book because of her religious beliefs. She told Blaine about the conversation her friend Bev had overheard between Sally and Susie.

"I've heard of Sally Lonsdale," Blaine said. "Your friend Bev's husband, Jim, mentioned to me one time that he plays golf with Sally's husband, Bob Lonsdale. He told Jim his wife had gone over the deep edge concerning anything related to the topic of sex. He said he was thinking of leaving her because she was obsessing over the subject, and although she'd always been quite religious and conservative, in the past few years she'd become almost rabid about the subject."

"I've met her a couple of times," Kat said, "but I can't say that I really know her. What I'm beginning to get concerned about is that my name and reputation are being drug through the mud, and that was even before I found Nancy lying dead on the floor in her office with a bullet hole in her chest. I can just imagine what they're going to say when they find out I was the one who discovered her body. Carl certainly thinks I'm guilty, and while I've always been a proponent of free speech, since that's what I always say when I get a bad review for my books being too close to erotica, I don't like Carl being able to tell everyone I should be arrested for killing his wife. That doesn't feel right to me."

"Kat, you know you can't stop people from talking. It's simply human nature. This will be a very juicy topic for people for quite some time, at least until the killer is caught. Once the murderer is arrested you'll become yesterday's news. Now, is there anyone else you can think of that might be considered as a suspect? So far we have Carl and Sally who possibly thought the only way to stop you was to murder Nancy."

"I find it hard to believe that Carl would even think of killing her. After all, he was her husband and the father of their daughter."

"I wish I could tell you those things don't happen, but the fact of the matter is they do, and with regularity. Actually, in a case like this two things are usually looked at first by police investigators. Number one is who has the most to gain by committing the murder. That would point to both Sally and Carl. Secondly, law enforcement usually looks to the spouse before they start with anyone else. Kat, I can see from your expression that something's going through your mind. What are you thinking?"

"I had a phone call this morning from someone who evidently felt threatened by my soon-to-be-published book. She said she could lose everything she had if the book was published because everyone would assume the female character in the book was her. She said her husband would divorce her, and she'd be banished from the Junior League. That fits into your scenario."

"Yes. Just tell me one thing. Is she a member of the country club?"

"Why do you ask?"

"Well," Blaine said, "The call I got this morning must have come from someone who saw us together last night. Other than that, there's no reason to assume we even know each other. Following that line of thought it has to be the wife of a golfer or a golfer herself, since the dinner was only open to the golf club members. Would that fit with the person who called you?"

Kat was quiet for a moment and then she said, "Yes. It certainly would, but I have no idea where to go with that information. I also know that Barbara, the gossipy dining room hostess at the country club, gave the woman a copy of my manuscript."

"Where did Barbara get it?" Blaine asked.

"Evidently it fell out of Nancy's tote bag when she was having lunch at the country club last week, and Barbara copied the manuscript and gave it to her."

"Kat, my brother's a private investigator. He's very good and very discreet. Although he does work all over the United States, he lives here in Lindsay, so he might be able to help clear your name and reputation. You could give him the names of Sally, Carl, and the other woman and see if he can come up with anything. While a lot of the private investigators today rely exclusively on computer searches for their information, he's pretty old-fashioned and likes to physically nose around and see what he can find out. Here's his phone number. If nothing else, it's a start. I'll tell him to keep his fee low as a favor to me," he said laughing as he handed her a card with his brother's contact information on it.

"Well, thanks to my books, money isn't quite the problem it was, but I appreciate saving money any way I can. If he can help clear my name, it will be money well spent."

Blaine stood up. "Kat, I don't quite know how to sugarcoat what I'm going to say, so I'll just say it straight out. I think you're in danger. Evidently there are at least three people who don't like the type of books you write, and quite possibly there are more than just those three. A woman has been murdered. We don't know if Nancy's murder is linked to your books, but it seems safe to say there may very well be a connection. Do you own a gun or have an alarm system here at the house?"

"I have an alarm system, but I usually never bother to set it. Lindsay is a pretty safe place to live, particularly in this area of town. Jazz is great about barking if anyone is on the property."

"Jazz is adorable, but if someone was intent on harming you, a ten-pound ball of fluff is not going to be a very good deterrent. Please, start setting your alarm. That might help. What about a gun?"

"Greg always kept one in the house. When he died I put it in a cabinet in the garage. It made me nervous. I was always afraid I might shoot Lacie if she came home unexpectedly. Oh dear, that reminds me. I've got to call her."

"Why don't you wait until I leave before you call her. I'd like to go out to the garage with you now and get the gun. Do you know how to shoot it?"

"Yes, when Greg got it he insisted I learn how to use it. We used to go to the gun range outside of town."

"Were you any good?" Blaine asked.

"Actually, I was very good. Greg thought I should enter some shooting competitions, but as I said before, guns make me nervous. I really don't want anything to do with them."

"Well, you're going to have to get over that. From now on you need to keep your gun with you at all times, even in your purse when you leave the house."

"Aren't you being a little melodramatic?" Kat asked.

"I don't think so. Now let's go out to the garage, and then I need to get back to the office and finish some work."

After Blaine left, she wondered if she should include the day's events in a book, and then decided no one would probably believe it, since it was literally stranger than fiction.

CHAPTER NINE

After the day she'd had, Kat decided she needed to give herself some tender loving care in the form of comfort food. For her that meant fixing clam linguini. She didn't know why it always worked for her, but it did. She knew everyone had their favorite comfort food and very simply, clam linguini was hers. She remembered Bev's response when she'd told her once that the dish was her favorite go-to comfort food. She smiled as she recalled Bev's shocked expression and then her words, "You've got to be kidding! Chicken soup I can understand, ice cream I can understand, brownies I can understand, but clam linguini as a comfort food? That I can't understand. Kat, having clam linguini as a comfort food is about the strangest thing I've ever heard. If I were you, I think I'd keep it to myself."

Later, after she'd cleaned up the last of her dirty dishes, Kat walked over to her desk where she'd put Blaine's brother's business card. She pressed his telephone number into her cell phone. A moment later a man's voice said, "This is Nick Evans. May I help you?"

"Nick, my name is Kat Denham. Your brother gave me your telephone number and said you might be able to help me."

"I'll certainly try. What can I do for you?"

"Before I tell you, I'm wondering if private investigators have a code of ethics kind of like doctors and lawyers. I guess what I'm asking is when a client tells you something, is it confidential? I know that sounds pretty mangled, but this is the first time I've ever needed the services of a private investigator. Blaine thought I did, so that's why I'm calling you."

"If you know my brother at all, you know how ethical and honest he is. I'd like to say I have the same standards. As to whether or not the industry has standards I have to abide by, the answer is no. Do I have personal standards I feel compelled to abide by? The answer to that is yes. Whatever you tell me will be confidential. Let me ask you something before you begin. My wife is an English professor at the university. The head of the department for many years was a man named Greg Denham. Are you any relation to him?"

"Yes. I was his wife. As you probably know he died over two years ago in an automobile accident."

"I knew about the accident. My wife was very upset about it for a long time. Your husband was well-respected at the university. I'm sorry. Now, why don't you tell me why you called me?"

Kat told him everything that had happened since she'd been to Susie's Salon and ended with finding Nancy's body and calling his brother. She explained to him she was an author, and Nancy was her editor.

"Mrs. Denham, if you don't mind, I'd prefer to call you Kat. Is that all right with you?"

"Of course."

"Kat, I understand everything you've told me, but I'm still unclear as to what it is that you would like me to do for you."

"My reputation's at stake. The cat is out of the bag, so to speak, regarding the fact that I write under the pen name of Sexy Cissy. I can't do anything about that, and I'm sure what I write will be offensive to some people. What I need is help finding out who murdered Nancy. I need to clear my name. Her husband more or less accused me of murdering her. I don't want to be considered a suspect. The timing is not very good for people to find out that Sexy Cissy and I are one and the same, and also that I'm the one who found Nancy."

"I understand your concern. May I make a suggestion?" Nick asked.

"Of course. This is unchartered territory for me, so I'd appreciate any thoughts you might have."

"If you decide to hire me to investigate Nancy's murder, and I think that's what you're asking me to do, here's how I would go about it. I think we can work together. You know the people who are possible suspects, and I have ways of getting information about those people that aren't available to most people. I have a woman on my staff who's a genius at finding out things. I do a combination computer search as well as old-fashioned stake-outs as they are sometimes called. You mentioned three people, but you neglected to tell me the name of your caller. If I'm going to help you, I'll need that person's name."

"I'm reluctant to tell you because this person was worried that her husband, who's very well-known in Lindsay, would think she was the woman described in my new book who was having an affair. I believe the only reason she's worried is because she probably is in fact having an affair. Once I divulge her name, I'm essentially saying she is having an affair."

"Kat, I told you about my personal ethics. You will be the only person who has access to any information I discover. What you choose to do with it is up to you. I won't even say anything to Blaine."

She was quiet for a few minutes and then asked, "What is your fee for doing something like this?"

"I have a standard hourly fee of $150. The hourly rate is for anything I do associated with the case. It might be a computer search, a stakeout, telephone calls, anything. The only additional expenses would be costs that I incur in connection with the case such as long distance calls, mileage, and things of that nature. I require a $1,500 retainer to be paid before I start the case. Once that's used up, if more work is necessary, I will bill you on a weekly basis."

"That sounds fair. How would you like me to pay?"

"I have a PayPal account, and you can pay through that. It's easier than checks or credit cards. Just give me your email address, and I'll send you an invoice. Actually, this is perfect timing. I just completed a case for a woman who wanted to know if her husband was having an affair. He was, and she's deciding what to do with the information I gave her, so I can get started on your case immediately. Although you told me what happened to you today, you didn't tell me the names of the people I'll be investigating, so let's start with those."

"Nancy's husband's name is Carl Jennings. I don't know much about him or where he's originally from, but I believe he's lived here in Lindsay for quite a few years. I've run into him several times over the years at various meetings and events. As I mentioned earlier, he's very rigid in his thinking about anything with a sexual connotation attached to it. The woman's name is Sally Lonsdale. She's the one who told my hairdresser she was amazed that I would even show up in church after writing the type of books I write. She's very religious and very active in the Calvary Baptist Church in town."

"Do you know if she's from the area?"

"I'm pretty sure she is. I've been going to the Lindsay Episcopal Church off and on for years. It's located right next door to the Baptist Church, and every time I've been there I've seen Sally going in or out of the Baptist Church. I believe she and Carl are good friends. He and Nancy attended the church as well, although from what Nancy told me, he is far more religious than she was."

"All right, that's two of them. What about the woman who called you?"

"Her name is Tiffany Conners. She's a regular at the country club. When Greg was alive we went to the club quite often, and she was always there, usually in the bar. I don't think she's from around here. She married Nelson Conners about five years ago. She's what some would call a 'trophy wife.' You know, quite a bit younger than he is, actually about twenty-five years younger. She's very attractive, and the talk around town is that most of what you see when you look at her has been implanted or enhanced by a plastic surgeon. Does that help?"

"Yes. I'll get started and give you a call in the morning with what I've been able to find out. You've had a rough day, try and get some sleep. I take a personal interest in my clients and based on what you've told me tonight, I think you need to be very, very careful until the killer is caught. I hope you have an alarm system and a gun."

"I have both, and you sound just like your brother," she said laughing. "I also have a dog that is great at alerting me when anything unusual is going on."

"Dogs are a good thing to have at a time like this. What breed is it?" he asked.

"A West Highland Terrier, and don't say anything. Your brother already has."

"The only thing I'm going to say is that you might check out buying a Rottweiler in the morning. Westies are cute little dogs, but as guard dogs, I don't think so."

"I'll keep it in mind. Thanks. Let me give you my email address."

A few minutes later they ended the call. She turned on the outside back yard lights and gingerly opened the door for Jazz to go out one more time. She mentally berated herself for being afraid when she looked out into the yard at the shadows where the lights couldn't reach. As she set the alarm system, she thought *Maybe Blaine and Nick are right. Maybe I should get a Rottweiler. I don't seem to be doing so well by myself.*

CHAPTER TEN

Kat spent a sleepless night tossing and turning. The first rays of the morning sun had just spilled through the slats of her louvered bedroom windows when she heard the front door open. She couldn't figure out why the alarm hadn't gone off. Her heart beat rapidly as she quietly opened the drawer of her nightstand and took the gun out. She looked down at Jazz who was wagging her tail. Just as she swung her legs over the side of the bed she heard Lacie's voice saying, "Mom, it's me. I wanted to talk to you before I went to class today. Where are you?"

"I'm in the bedroom. Be right with you." She quickly put the gun back in the drawer, knowing it would frighten Lacie if she saw it and also knowing Lacie would question why Kat felt she needed to keep a gun in her nightstand. Evidently Lacie had turned off the alarm when she'd come in.

A few minutes later Kat walked into the kitchen where Lacie was making coffee. She turned and faced Kat, "Mom, I want to apologize for last night. I was out of line, and I feel really bad about our conversation."

Kat walked over and put her arms around Lacie. "Honey, I understand. You've been worried for a long time about people finding out that I write the Sexy Cissy books, but Lacie, look at it this way. People don't have to buy them. There are some sex scenes, I grant you that, but there isn't any violence or people speaking filth. As a matter of fact, I get a lot of fan mail from people who really like my books. They're quick reads, and they bring a little enjoyment into the lives of a lot of people. At least that's how I look at it. Plus, it's certainly allowed us to live a far better life than we'd able to if I was working in a fast food restaurant somewhere, struggling to keep us in this house."

"I know, Mom, it was just a lot of things. Nicole's father and uncle came to the sorority house yesterday afternoon and told her about her mother being murdered. Her room is next to mine, and I heard her screaming at her father."

"You're kidding!" Kat said. "Why would she do that? I mean it had to have been a terrible blow to Carl and Nicole."

"She was screaming something about it all being his fault for getting so mad at her mother for editing the Sexy Cissy books. He yelled back that maybe Nicole's mother deserved to die for editing filth like that. Then it got real quiet, and I could hear Nicole crying. Her father tried to take her home, but she refused to go with him. She said she couldn't sleep in the same house where her mother had been murdered."

"Oh, that poor child. I feel so sorry for her," Kat said. "This is a time when she and her father need to support each other."

"Mom, Nicole didn't know you were Sexy Cissy. She heard her father and mother arguing about her mother editing those books, but she didn't know the books they were arguing about were the books you'd written. Her father told her mother she better stop editing those books, or he'd make sure she did. Her mother told him his attitude towards sex was sick, and since she was an adult, she'd make up her own mind about what books she chose to edit."

"How did you find that out, Lacie?" Kat asked.

"Nicole and I have become very good friends. After you and I talked last night, or rather after I hung up on you, and again I'm sorry, it was just that I'd always been so afraid people would find out you were Sexy Cissy, and I was afraid I might even get kicked out of the sorority because of it. Anyway, I realized you were more important to me than the sorority, and actually, based on what a couple of people told me last night, no one really cared. One person said it was a much better profession than selling people houses or cars or other things they knew the buyer couldn't afford, just so they could make a profit. When I thought about it, I realized they were right."

"I'm glad, Lacie. I've never felt ashamed about what I write, but I also didn't see any reason to alert people that I was the author of a type of a book they might find offensive. If they choose to read one of my books, it's their choice, not mine."

"Back to Nicole. I waited about an hour, and then I knocked on her door. I felt so sorry for her. I know she and her mother were close, and her death had to be a horrible shock to Nicole. I mean, it's bad enough to have your mother die, but to have your father threaten your mother, and then to have her murdered. She told me she was afraid her father had done something terrible. She couldn't bring herself to say he killed Mrs. Jennings, but she certainly implied it. She said her mother had told her once that Sexy Cissy was a really good writer. Nicole wondered if that was her real name. Mom, I told her you were Sexy Cissy."

"Oh, honey, are you sure that was a wise thing to do?"

"Well, after you told me last night that several people at the club knew, it was just a matter of time before she heard it. I thought it would be better if she heard it from me. She was very surprised and told me she thought the author would be some sex queen looking person, not an ordinary mother. I told her how I was always afraid people would find out about it, and I was almost ashamed of it. I'm sorry, Mom, but I'm just being honest."

"Lacie, I wouldn't have you any other way. It sounds like you were able to help her."

"I think just talking to me helped. She wasn't at all judgmental about you. As a matter of fact, she asked me if she could stay here at our house during Christmas break, because she didn't want anything to do with her father."

"Oh boy. I don't know how good of an idea that is. Her father hates me enough without me taking his daughter from him. Let's think about it."

"Mom, please, Nicole is really suffering. She doesn't need you to reject her. I told her I was going to talk to you this morning."

Kat was quiet for several moments and then said, "Let me think about it, but I'm pretty sure her father isn't going to be very happy about this."

"Well, Nicole is eighteen, and in this state I believe she can legally make up her own mind whether she wants to stay at home or not, and she doesn't want to stay at home. I'll tell her you're thinking about it, and there's a good chance she can stay with us during the holidays."

Maybe I should get the Rottweiler. I have no idea what Carl will do when he finds this out, and if he is the killer, I could be in real danger. Better if Lacie doesn't even think of that possibility.

"To change the subject," Kat said. "Remember when you were a kid I'd sometimes make that special coffee cake for you and dad on the weekends? The one with lots of brown sugar? Got time for me to make it for you now?"

"Of course I remember. I've got two hours before my first class, so that should be plenty of time. Yes, definitely make it."

Forty-five minutes later Lacie said, "Mom, are you expecting someone? It's pretty early for guests." She walked to the front door to see who had rung the doorbell.

"No, I'm not expecting anyone and please find out who it is before you open the door," Kat said as she took the coffee cake out of the oven. Kat hadn't wanted to alarm Lacie and other than telling her about finding Nancy, she had deliberately chosen not to tell her the other things that had happened yesterday.

"Mom, it's Blaine Evans, the District Attorney you went out with. Okay with you if I let him in?"

"Of course," Kat said, running her hands through her hair and mentally chastising herself for not having at least put on some lipstick and running a mascara wand over her lashes. She smoothed her robe and smiled at Blaine as he walked into the kitchen.

"Good morning, Blaine, I see you've met my daughter, Lacie. She came over for an early breakfast. I just took a coffee cake out of the oven. Care to join us?"

"I'd love to. Thanks," he said pulling out a chair from the kitchen table. "I'd also take a cup of that coffee I can smell." He turned to Lacie, who had seated herself at the table. "I understand you're a junior at the university. What are you studying?"

"I'm majoring in psychology. I hope to become a psychologist and work with teenagers. I don't know why it appeals to me, but having just gotten out of my teens, I know how difficult those years can be. I really would like to help some of them, particularly those less fortunate than I was. I had a mom and a dad who were always there for me."

"That's admirable, and I'm sure you will make a difference." He turned to Kat and said, "This may be the best coffee cake I've ever eaten. I'm beginning to think you're a woman of many talents."

"Thanks. Glad you're enjoying it. Lacie, why don't you wrap up the rest of the coffee cake and take it with you? You can have some tomorrow morning or maybe share it with Nicole. She could probably use some comfort food about now." She turned to Blaine and said, "That's Nancy's daughter. She and Lacie are quite good friends. As a matter of fact, they have rooms next to each other in the sorority house."

"Kat, Lacie, I would love to stay and talk to both of you, but I'm due in court in a little while." He turned to Kat. "My brother called me last night. He and I both think you need to get a dog that's a little more threatening than Jazz. He has a very good friend who trains Rottweilers for the police, and he called him. His friend said he has the perfect dog for you. It's a one-year-old male. He's a fully trained guard dog that loves other dogs and prefers women to men. I'd really appreciate it if you would go out to his kennel, sooner rather than later, and take a look at the dog. By the way, if you decide you want to bring him home with you, his fee has been taken care of," Blaine said with a twinkle in his eye.

"Mom, you never mentioned getting another dog, and why a Rottweiler? I mean aren't those scary, dangerous dogs?"

Kat looked from Blaine to Lacie. "Lacie, Blaine is worried that because Nancy was murdered, and she was my editor, I could possibly be in danger. I'm certain I'm not, but living alone it probably wouldn't be a bad idea for me to have a dog that's a little more threatening than Jazz."

"If it makes you more comfortable, I'm all for it, but if you get one, I'd appreciate it if you would introduce him to me, so I don't have a problem when I want to come home from time to time."

"I'll make sure you're properly introduced. Blaine, I don't know what district attorneys are paid, but I definitely can afford to buy my own dog."

"Kat, we haven't had time to tell our stories to each other. As a matter of fact, something you'll find out about me sooner or later is that I come from blue blood, old Kansas City stock," he said laughing. "Not that anyone cares about that stuff anymore, certainly not my brother or me."

"Blue blood? What do you mean?"

"Well, years ago there was a thing called the Blue Book of Kansas City, kind of a social register for the upper class, so to speak. My family was in it for years. When the editor decided the cost of printing it was getting too expensive, and it should be borne by the families who were listed in it, he asked them for a donation. My grandmother was furious and told him she'd never pay to be included in it. She felt it was her birthright. That was the end of the Evans family in the Blue Book.

"You'll also probably find out my family had some money, actually quite a lot of money. Originally it came from a five-thousand-acre wheat farm and cattle ranch my family owned in western Kansas. Around 1950 the family discovered that the ranch was smack dab in the middle of the famous Hugoton oil and gas field which covers a large area of western Kansas. Today the Hugoton field is the 5th largest source of natural gas in the United States with approximately eleven thousand oil and gas wells operating in it.

"Around five hundred of those wells are located on the ranch property owned by my family. Before we struck oil, the ranch was doing quite well financially, but the money really started rolling in with the discovery of oil on the property.

"Money's never been that important to me or my brother even though we each inherited a large trust fund. Both of our funds kind of sit there, doing nothing. No, that's not true. Actually, both of us are big donors to a number of non-profit organizations whose names I won't bother to bore you with. Bottom line is, I can well afford to buy you a gift."

"Well, I don't know what to say except I hope you won't mind if I put your grandmother in one of my books. Actually, I'd like to hear more about your family."

"Kat, my grandmother would have been the star of one of your books. I always thought she was feisty and independent enough that she might very well have had a secret life of her own that was very interesting and none of us knew about. I was pretty young, so I never heard the juicy parts, but I'm sure there were a lot. Anyway, I really do have to leave. Here's the kennel guy's information. I'll call you later and see how you and Rudy, that's the dog's name, are getting along."

"Blaine, I don't recall saying I was going to get Rudy."

"Don't think you did, but I know you meant to," he grinned as he walked towards the front door. "Nice meeting you, Lacie. Look forward to seeing you again. Maybe later today when we both meet Rudy." He closed the door behind him and walked to his car.

"Mom, I know it's none of my business, but you might want to think about developing a relationship with Blaine. It looks to me like you must have made some kind of an impression on him. He's a lawyer, he's the district attorney, he's single, he's rich, he's attractive, and he bought you a dog. What's not to like about him?"

"Well, at the moment, nothing, but I really know very little about him."

"Mom, as I recall you told me you married dad six weeks after you met him. I doubt you knew very much about him, but that seemed to work, didn't it?"

"Yes, sweetheart, it did. You need to get on your way, or you'll be late for class. Here's the coffee cake and Lacie, thanks for stopping by this morning."

"I'm glad I did. I love you, Mom."

CHAPTER ELEVEN

After assuring Lacie she'd be the first to know if Kat decided to buy a Rottweiler dog, she walked her to the door and again told Lacie how glad she was that she'd stopped by. She closed the door and stood next to it for a moment, thankful she was able to have such a good relationship with her daughter and sorry that Carl and Nicole didn't get along. With Nancy dead, she felt something must be done to heal their relationship because they only had each other. The ringing phone jolted her out of her reverie. Answering it she said, "Hello, this is Kat."

"Good morning, Kat. I hope I'm not calling too early. This is Nick. I did quite a bit of research last night, actually into the early morning hours, and I'd like to share with you what I've found out so far on the case. At the moment I'm on a stakeout down the street from Tiffany Conners' home. I'm curious about her."

"Nick, I've been up for hours, so you're definitely not calling too early. I barely slept at all last night, and then my daughter came over from the university very early this morning, followed by your brother. I understand the two of you have decided I need to get a Rottweiler dog for protection, and you've already contacted a friend of yours who specializes in breeding them and training them for law enforcement personnel. I was just getting ready to call him when the phone rang. I'd love to hear what you've found out so far."

"I'll start with Carl Jennings. I'm no psychologist, but I have a pretty good idea why he hates your books so much and why he didn't want Nancy to be your editor. His parents lived in the small town of Montezuma, Kansas. His father was the mayor of the town and owned the only car dealership for miles around. He was quite successful and was a pillar of the community. His mother was from a small nearby town. She was the homecoming queen in high school and a cheerleader while she was in college. According to what I read about her and the pictures I saw, she was extremely attractive. When Carl was growing up, she stayed at home to raise him. She'd gotten a degree as a physical therapist when she was in college, but never used it. Because Carl's father was quite well off financially, he didn't want his wife to work."

"None of that sounds all that unusual," Kat said.

"That part wasn't the least bit unusual. It would have been more unusual if the mayor's wife had worked, particularly when he was the owner of a successful car dealership. What was unusual was when she left her husband for a car salesman who worked for him, and the two of them moved to Wichita. She got a job as a physical therapist, and he worked as a car salesman. After her relationship with him turned sour, his mother lived with a different man almost on a yearly basis. For several years Carl's father hoped she'd return to him and Carl, but it never happened. Every year Carl's father hired a private investigator to find out where she was and who she was living with.

"Finally he realized she was never coming back to them, and he divorced her. Unfortunately, his legacy to his son was to constantly tell him what a bad woman his mother was. Evidently he told Carl he'd found all kinds of sexy novels in her desk drawers after she'd left. There's documentation that his father told a number of people in the small town where he and Carl lived that the reason his wife left him was because she believed all the stuff she read in the tawdry novels. After she left, Carl's father became quite religious and told everyone what a sinner his wife was, and that when she died she would surely burn in the fires of hell for the sinful life she'd led."

"Nick, that would sure explain why Carl was so adamant about

Nancy not editing my books. They're not that trashy, and a lot of people think they're very well written, but that must have been what his thinking was. He was probably afraid Nancy would leave him just as his mother had left his father. Poor man. I almost feel sorry for him."

"I agree that it probably explains why he's so opposed to books such as the ones you write, but it still doesn't mean he didn't kill his wife. The whole thing could have gotten so twisted in his mind that he might have believed he needed to kill her to keep her, if you know what I mean."

"Nick, here's another piece of information I just found out from my daughter this morning. She lives in the Pi Beta Phi sorority house on the university campus, and Carl's daughter, Nicole, is one of her closest friends. Nicole doesn't want anything to do with her father, and she asked my daughter if she could stay at our house during the upcoming holidays. I can certainly imagine how that's going to sit with Carl, and it's not going to be good."

"Again, I'm not a psychologist, but if he's as strongly opposed to sexy novels as we think, and if he murdered his wife to keep her from leaving him, he might just do the same to his daughter to keep her. What did you tell your daughter about letting Nicole stay with you during the holidays?"

"I said I'd have to think about it and let her know."

"And what do you think about it?"

"I'm vacillating, but I probably will let her stay here. If Carl's somewhat deranged, she'd probably be safer here at my house than at hers, particularly if I get the Rottweiler."

"Kat, I'm going to have to call you back. Tiffany just opened her garage door and is backing out. I want to follow her. I found out some information about her I think you'll find interesting. Call my friend and get the dog."

"I'll call him now, and I'm really curious to know what you found out about Tiffany."

"I'll get back to you as soon as I can," Nick said ending the conversation.

CHAPTER TWELVE

Using her cell phone, Kat pressed in the phone number Blaine had given her for the kennel. A moment later he heard a male voice say, "Casey's Kennels, may I help you?"

"I believe so. My name is Kat Denham. A friend of yours, Nick Evans, strongly suggested I talk to you about buying one of your Rottweiler dogs. He said you have one that's a year old and is very friendly towards women. I believe he told me the dog's name is Rudy. Actually Nick's brother is the one who told me about you, but Nick confirmed the dog's name is Rudy when I talked to him this morning. Can you tell me something about the breed? I have a Westie now, and I've never owned a large dog like a Rottweiler."

"Kat, I'm very prejudiced about the breed. Sometimes they get a bad rap for being too aggressive, but I personally believe it's because they haven't been properly trained, and they don't know any better. These are very strong dogs, and they need to be socialized when they're young. I don't sell any of them until they're at least a year old. While I train them to be guard dogs, they are also part of my family, so they're used to children as well as adults.

"The breed is protective and considers the home where they live and property they're on to be part of the area that needs to be protected. Unless the resident of the home invites someone in and is friendly towards them, Rottweilers don't like to have strangers on their property. My dogs only attack when they are given a command to do so. I feel confident enough with the breed that I have no problem with them being in the house with my two boys who are very young. By the way, my wife loves the breed, and she's particularly fond of Rudy."

"Do they need special exercising or things like that, since they're guard dogs?" Kat asked.

"No, but I wouldn't want to see them try and acclimate themselves to a small apartment or condominium with no yard. They're big dogs and need some exercise, but usually just being outdoors for a period of time will be enough for them. While they appear very threatening to others, as I said earlier, they don't attack without provocation or a command being given to them."

"Since I have a small dog, the Westie I mentioned, could a Rottweiler co-exist with her?"

"Yes. As I said, my dogs are totally socialized. Since I sell almost exclusively to law enforcement personnel they have to be trained to get along with other dogs and people. They are pretty much one person or one family dogs. In other words, the dogs have an owner who is employed in law enforcement. They're not the property of the police agency. They like to bond with their owners. If you'd like, I can set up a time for you to meet Rudy and see if he's what you're thinking about getting."

"Casey, I'll be very honest. Until Nick's brother turned up on my doorstep this morning and told me he was giving me Rudy as a gift, other than an occasional fleeting thought that I might need a guard dog since I live alone, I never dreamed I'd even think of owning a large dog like a Rottweiler. Now it looks like it's going to be a reality. Could you see me this afternoon? And lastly, if Rudy and I get along, could I take him with me?"

"Yes, if you like him, he can go home with you. I could see you at 2:30 this afternoon. Will that work for you?"

"That would be fine. I have your address, and I understand your kennel is about half an hour from town. I'll see you then. If you need to get in touch with me, here's my number."

Kat ended the call and sat for a moment, thinking how her life had changed in the last twenty-four hours. She'd discovered Nancy's body, been outed as writing under the pen name of Sexy Cissy, accused of causing Nancy's death by Carl, began a relationship with Blaine, and now she was probably going to bring home a Rottweiler for protection. She sat for a moment, amazed at everything that had happened. She slowly shook her head from side to side in disbelief and then called the district attorney's office. She asked the receptionist if she could speak with Blaine Evans and gave the receptionist her name.

A moment later she heard Blaine's voice. "To what do I owe the pleasure of this call?" he asked warmly.

"I'm reporting in. I have an appointment at 2:30 to meet Rudy, the Rottweiler you're giving me. I thought you should be the first to know."

"Thanks, Kat," he said in a somber tone. "I'm worried about you living alone given everything that's happened. Actually, I was just about to call you. The judge became ill this morning and had to adjourn court. I have some unexpected free time. How about meeting me for lunch at the country club? If you'd like, I can go out to the kennel with you."

"That would be wonderful. Casey said I could bring Rudy home with me if I wanted to, but I was wondering how I was physically going to do that. What time do you want me to meet you?"

"It's 10:30 now. Let's say 12:30. That will give us time to have a leisurely lunch and then drive out to the kennel. I've never been there, and Nick has talked so much about it, I'd like to see it. We can take my car from the club. I saw your car yesterday and it might be a bit tight with you, me, and Rudy in it. I understand they're pretty big dogs."

"That sounds great. I definitely would like to go in your car. Driving with a big dog would really be a first for me. I could probably use a dry run in your car."

"Consider it done. I'll see you at 12:30."

CHAPTER THIRTEEN

Kat opened her closet and stood for a few moments debating what the possible future owner of a guard dog should wear that would also be appropriate for having lunch with the man who was giving her the guard dog. She wanted to look good because she had to admit she had more than a passing interest in Blaine. She finally decided on a pair of herringbone slacks and a dark blue sweater with a cowl neckline.

She didn't know if Rottweilers shed much, but if they did, pants that were a single color probably wouldn't work well. It had turned cold overnight, and she thought she better wear her heavy camel colored wool coat which she only wore in the dead of winter. The weatherman had predicted the change in temperature, and on the morning news she'd listened to him talking about an approaching snowstorm.

She drove the short distance to the country club, parked in the lot, and walked up the steps. When she opened the door and saw the Christmas trees and their twinkling lights, it reminded her that Lacie wanted Nicole to spend the Christmas break at their home rather than be with her father.

I just don't feel comfortable with that. If I was Carl and it was my daughter, I'd be very hurt and very angry. I really don't know how I'm going to handle it.

Kat saw Blaine sitting at a corner table waiting for her, looking very handsome in a grey pinstripe suit. She waved to him and held up a finger indicating she'd be there in just a moment. When she'd walked into the restaurant she'd seen Barbara standing at the hostess station and decided to ask her if anyone else had a copy of the lost manuscript for The Country Club Cover-Up.

"Good afternoon, Barbara. How are you today?"

"I'm fine, Mrs. Denham. What's the occasion? I haven't seen you in ages and now you're here two days in a row."

"Well, as you know, I met my good friend Bev yesterday, and I'm meeting my friend Blaine today. If you have a moment, I'd like to ask you a couple of questions."

"I'm all yours until someone comes in. What can I help you with?" Barbara asked.

"You told me that Nancy Jennings was here for lunch last week, and you found a manuscript with a note from me attached to it under the table where she'd been seated. You also told me you copied it and had given a copy of the manuscript to Sally Lonsdale and Tiffany Conners. Did you give anyone else a copy?"

"No, like I told you I went in the office and made a copy for Sally and then later I made one for Tiffany."

"Wasn't the club manager curious as to why you were copying something that had so many pages?"

Barbara looked down at her fingernails and then up at Kat. "Please don't say anything to anyone. The club manager was gone for the day. I didn't think anyone would ever find out. I made two copies, like I told you, one for each of them. If the manager finds out, I'll lose my job, and I can't afford to be out of work. My husband, Johnnie, lost his job a month ago, and it's a bad time of year to find a new one. Please Mrs. Denham, don't say anything. We really need the money I make here at the club."

"I won't say anything, but I'm wondering if you returned the original manuscript to Mrs. Jennings."

"Not exactly. Her husband was in here for lunch the day after I'd copied the manuscript, so I gave it to him to give to her. I hope that was okay to do. Now that she's dead, I suppose it doesn't matter."

"Actually, that probably explains a lot of things. Don't worry, Barbara, your secret is safe with me, and I hope Johnnie finds work soon. Thanks for being honest with me."

"Thank you, Mrs. Denham." Her voice clearly conveyed her relief.

*****

"Sorry to keep you waiting," Kat said a moment later to Blaine, as he stood up from the table and helped her take off her coat. "I needed to ask Barbara a couple of things."

"From the serious looks on both of your faces, I hope your questions were answered."

"Yes, although I'm not sure it helps me a lot. It might actually make things more difficult."

Kat spent the next few moments looking at the menu. "Well," Blaine said, "what's your lunch decision?"

She put the menu on the table and said, "With the weather as cold as it is outside and snow on the way, I can't get past the open-faced gourmet chili on honey cornbread. That sounds wonderful."

"I agree." He looked up at the waiter who had walked over to their table. "Vic, we'd both like the open-faced chili on honey cornbread. Will you vouch for it?" Blaine asked, smiling up at the waiter.

"Absolutely, sir. It's my favorite. Matter of fact I have it almost every day after I'm finished with the lunch crowd. It should be out in a few minutes. Would you like a salad to go with it?"

"Not for me," Kat said.

"Me neither," Blaine said. "I had a great coffee cake for breakfast and the chili will be plenty. Thanks, Vic."

Blaine leaned across the table and said, "I understand Nick called you this morning. I called to tell him that I'd spoken with Casey at the kennel, and you were going to make an appointment with him for today. He mentioned that he'd gotten in touch with one of his employees who's a computer whiz and between them they'd found out quite a bit. Nick is very, very ethical, and I knew he wouldn't tell me what he'd found out, so I didn't even bother to ask. Naturally my curiosity is on high alert. Would you care to tell me what he found out?"

"Sure, although we had to cut the conversation short. Here's what he had to say about Carl Jennings." She relayed what Nick had found out about him.

"Poor guy. Sounds like he had a lousy childhood, and it sure explains why he acted like he did yesterday. It's a good thing he has his daughter. They're going to have to rely on each other in the coming weeks."

"Blaine, that would be true in an ideal situation, but this is not an ideal situation."

She looked over at Vic who was walking towards their table carrying two plates piled high with chili over cornbread. On the sides of each large plate were two small dishes, one contained chopped onions and the other was filled with shredded cheese. "May I get anything else for you?" Vic asked.

"Yes, I'd like some red pepper flakes," Blaine said. He looked over at Kat whose eyes were open wide in amazement.

"Don't you think you ought to try it first and see how spicy it is before you add red pepper to it?" she asked.

"Probably, but I like my food as spicy as I can get it, excluding things like coffee cake."

Kat grinned and said, "Next time I'll put jalapeño peppers in it. As a matter of fact, it might be kind of good fixed that way. It certainly would be different. Let's eat this while it's hot, and then I'll tell you about the quandary I'm in concerning what to do about Carl's daughter."

They were quiet for several minutes simply enjoying their meal. When Blaine was finished eating, he said, "Looks like you're almost finished. I'd like to hear what happened."

She told him about her conversation with Lacie, and how Lacie had asked Kat if Nicole could spend the Christmas holiday break at their home because she didn't want anything to do with her father.

"What did you tell her?" Blaine asked, buttering a piece of cornbread that had escaped being smothered with chili.

"I told her I'd have to think about it. Blaine, I just found out from Barbara that she gave my manuscript, you know the one I told you that fell out of Nancy's tote bag, to Carl so he could return it to Nancy. I think he must have read it, and that's why he was so angry with me the night I met you and yesterday when we were at his house after I'd discovered Nancy's body."

"That would make perfect sense. Did Nancy ever mention whether or not she'd told Carl she was editing your books?"

"Not exactly. I think I told you that she'd laughed one time about none of my books being displayed in her bookcase, because all of the other books she'd edited were prominently displayed in her bookcase after they'd been published. She said something to the effect that Carl probably wouldn't approve of them."

"Given what you've told me about his background, I'm sure she was right. Back to the Christmas break quandary. Are you leaning more towards taking Nicole in or telling her you can't?"

"I go back and forth. She's over eighteen, and as I understand it, neither her father nor a judge can legally force her to go to Carl's house if she doesn't want to. Isn't that true?"

"Yes, you'd be on firm ground legally, but given how he feels about you, I'm sure your home is the last place where he'd want his daughter to spend the holidays."

"I agree, Blaine, and that's why I have the appointment to see Rudy today. First of all, I'm sure Carl's going to be furious when he hears that his daughter might spend the holidays at my home. Secondly, we don't know for sure if he murdered his wife, but if he did, he also might consider murdering me."

"Think it's time we go meet Rudy and bring him home for you, but I do have a question for you."

"Shoot."

"Why couldn't I be interested in a woman who was attractive and intelligent, but wasn't involved in a murder case?" he asked, smiling at Kat.

"Don't know, Mr. District Attorney. Guess you'll have to answer that question yourself, but look at it this way. I don't recall you telling me that a guideline for a relationship with you was whether or not I'd bore you, and if you did ask me about that, I certainly didn't answer you. So look at it this way. I promise not to bore you." She grinned back at him. "Thanks for the compliment. Let's go check out Rudy."

"Give me the keys to your car. I'll stop by my office on the way and get someone to drive your car home."

"Thanks," Kat said. "I hadn't thought of that."

CHAPTER FOURTEEN

On the way to Casey's Kennels, Kat and Blaine talked of this and that. They laughed at the differences in their backgrounds. Kat grew up on a wheat farm near a small town twenty miles from the university. The farm had been in her father's family for generations. Her mother and dad made ends meet, but just barely. The only way Kat had been able to go to college was by getting a scholarship. She graduated from high school with a 4.0 grade average and that, along with her demonstrated financial need, qualified her for the scholarship which the university granted her.

Blaine grew up in Mission Hills, a wealthy suburb of Kansas City. His home had been in the family for generations, and his wealthy family had easily been able to afford to send him to college anywhere in the world he wanted to go. He'd chosen the nearby University of Kansas in Lawrence. After graduation he'd studied law at the University of Missouri at Kansas City. Once he'd been sworn in as a lawyer, he'd been recruited by several law firms who were familiar with his family's pedigree and their wealthy connections. A lot of law firms like to have a "rain maker" on their staff, a man who had those connections and could turn them into cash for the law firm.

When his fiancée died in a plane crash, he couldn't deal with the memories reminding him of her wherever he went in Kansas City. He'd moved to the small university town of Lindsay and joined the law practice of a friend he'd met in law school. Two years after Blaine moved to Lindsay his brother, Nick, had moved there.

Kat and Blaine readily agreed that their backgrounds couldn't have been more different, but here they were, thrown together by circumstances and each glad that circumstances had taken the turn they had. "Well, let's go meet this wonder dog Casey raved about last nigh--t. I hope he's everything he's supposed to be, and I'm not bringing you out to the kennel on some wild goose chase. You could be home writing the great American novel instead of meeting a guard dog," Blaine said smiling as they pulled into the parking lot of the kennel.

Blaine walked around the car and opened the door for Kat. "Thanks, Blaine," Kat said laughing as she got out of the car, "but I don't think the type of writing I do is ever going to qualify me for writing the great American novel."

She stepped onto the dirt parking lot and said, "Glad I wore boots. I did it more for the cold than anything else, but high heels in this dirt would have been a disaster." She stood for a moment looking at the long building where she assumed the dogs were housed. Next to it was a large two-story house.

"Bet that house has been here awhile. It looks like the type that was built in these parts around the early 20th century. I imagine the other building was originally a barn, and Casey added on to it. Let's go over to the house first," Blaine said.

As he knocked on the door she noticed the cheerful Christmas wreath that had been hung on it. It was quickly opened by a large man who appeared to be in his mid-30's. "You must be Kat, and I'm gathering this is Blaine. You certainly bear a resemblance to your brother. I'm Casey and welcome to my home. Please, come in."

They shook hands and were immediately surrounded by two little boys and three large dogs. "Daddy, daddy, is this the lady who's gonna take Rudy from us?"

"I don't know, Stefan. We'll have to wait and see. You know you and your brother get to make friends with all the puppies and watch them grow up. They'll never forget you. You could see them in ten years, and they'd still remember you." He turned to Kat. "He's pretty attached to Rudy. That's the dog sitting next to him. This happens every time one of them goes to their new owner. Usually I take them to whatever law enforcement agency has contracted with me for them, so I can spare the kids the separation pain. Probably should have done that today," he said looking at Stefan who had his arm circled tightly around Rudy's massive neck.

Kat knelt down and said, "Stefan, would you introduce me to Rudy? My name's Kat. You've done a beautiful job with Rudy. He's so calm and friendly."

Stefan looked her up and down debating whether or not she was good enough for his friend, Rudy. Finally, a decision was made and he said, "Rudy, this is Kat. She's the one I told you about." Kat turned to the big black dog with one mahogany dot above each eye on the inner brow ridge, another dot on his cheeks, and a mahogany strip on each side of his nose. He was beautiful and wagged his tail in greeting. Kat put her hand out so the big dog could sniff it and said, "Hi, Rudy, nice to meet you." She stood up and turned to Casey. "Since I've never done anything like this, what do I need to know about him?"

"I've prepared an information packet for you. I figured you'd want him. Out of all the dogs I've raised in the last ten years, he may be the best. He's highly intelligent, and he loves my wife. She couldn't meet you, because she's become so attached to him she knew she'd start crying when she had to say goodbye to him. All of the words he's familiar with are described in the packet as well as some hand gestures you should memorize. I would suggest you keep him inside your house, even at night. My understanding is that you need a guard dog, and if he's in a kennel in a garage he wouldn't be very effective trying to guard you. It actually would cause him a great deal of anxiety if there was a situation when he needed to guard you, and he was unable to do so because he was locked in a kennel."

"I'm fine with that. Does he need a dog bed or a crate or what?"

"I have everything you'll need for him. It's all in the barn and included in his price. He knows his own smells and sometimes dogs get a little spooked when they're in a new environment and not only is everything strange to them, they don't even have their kennels or dog beds that they're used to. I also have enough food for him for several days as well as a collar and a heavy duty leash. Naturally he's housebroken and leash trained. About the only thing you'll have to do is get an ID tag for him with your contact information on it. You can do that online and have it sent to you."

"I told you I have a female Westie at home who's been spayed. What's the best way to introduce them?"

"Has the Westie done much socializing with other dogs?"

"A lot. I'm an author, and I think better when it's quiet in the house. For the last year I've taken Jazz, that's my dog's name, to a dog day care center two days a week. She plays with the other dogs, and from what the attendants have told me, she's a model dog and gets along very well with the other dogs."

"Then you shouldn't have any problems. I would suggest putting Rudy in the back yard, if you have one, and let your Westie find him. That way the Westie won't feel that her space has been intruded on. I take it from these questions you'll be taking Rudy with you."

"Was there ever any doubt?" Kat asked laughing.

"Not in my mind," Casey replied. "Let's go out to the barn and get his things. I'll bring his leash in, and then you can walk him out to the car.

"In a moment," Kat said, kneeling in front of Stefan. "Stefan, you've done such a good job raising Rudy, I want to thank you. I hope your dad will bring you to my house once in a while, so you two could have a play day with Rudy. I'm sure Rudy would like that."

"Daddy, daddy, can we?" Stefan asked, jumping up and down.

Casey put his big hand on Stefan's head and said, "Absolutely. Look at it this way, Rudy's not leaving. You're just lending him to Kat. She needs him now. Understand?"

"Yep. Can we go tomorrow?" Stefan asked.

"I think we better wait a couple of days for Rudy to get used to Kat and his new sister. Kat has another dog, so Rudy needs a little time to get to know her. Okay?"

"Yeah, just so I can go see him. Bye, Rudy, see you in a few days." He kissed Rudy on his head and walked into the family room to join his brother who was watching cartoons.

"Thank you, Kat. I really appreciate what you just did. This is always the hardest time for all of us. You made it easy," Casey said.

"I meant everything I said. I'll look forward to seeing you and Stefan sometime soon."

After they returned from the barn Casey put the leash on Rudy and handed it to Kat. "Let's get this over with," he said opening the door and walking towards Blaine's car with a hint of wetness in his eyes.

CHAPTER FIFTEEN

Blaine loaded the crate, the dog bed, the food, and everything else that Casey gave him into his SUV. Kat petted Rudy and talked to him while Blaine finished up. A few minutes later they waved goodbye to Casey and drove to Rudy's new home.

"Blaine, I can't thank you enough for buying Rudy for me, although, as I told you, I certainly could have bought him myself. I think he and I have bonded. I just hope he and Jazz will get along together."

"First of all you're very welcome. Actually, buying him for you was selfish on my part because last night I realized I liked you a lot and didn't want anything to happen to you." He turned to her and said, "It surprised the heck out of me, but hey, maybe it's time for me to finally let go of the past and move on. I went to see a therapist years ago, and he told me that's what I needed to do in order to get over Jessie's death. Guess he was right, although I didn't realize I hadn't moved on until I met you."

"You've had a few more years to heal than I have, but I think I'm ready to move on as well," Kat said. "Maybe we just met at the right time, that or the stars were aligned perfectly, although astrology never particularly interested me. My friend Bev is a huge believer in it. She goes to Kansas City to see someone she says is the best astrologer in the Midwest to have her astrology chart done for the coming year. I can't tell you how many times over the years she wouldn't do one thing or another because of the chart that was drawn up for her for that year. That stuff kind of makes me feel like I don't have any control over my life, and I'd like to think I do, but I know a number of people who read what's in the newspaper about their sign every day and really are believers in it."

"I didn't know that about Bev. Jim's never mentioned it, and I have to agree with you, although I really know next to nothing about it."

"The reason Jim's never mentioned it is because she doesn't discuss it with him. She told me once that she knew Jim wouldn't approve of her going to Kansas City for her annual chart check-up, as she calls it, so she tells him she has to go to Kansas City to go shopping. She generally goes in early December, and she does do some Christmas shopping, so technically she's not lying to Jim. More of an absence of telling him everything. Actually, she went last week and she told me her astrologer said the coming year was going to be one of the best she'd ever had."

She inhaled deeply and said, "Blaine, I know I'm changing the subject, but I'm really nervous about Jazz and Rudy. I mean, what am I going to do if they don't get along?"

He looked over at her and smiled. "Looks like I'll just have to take one of them home. They're both nice dogs, and I've been thinking for a long time that I might like to have a dog. Let's see what happens. Have you decided how you're going to introduce them?"

"I've been thinking about it, and I'm going to let Rudy out in the back yard, and Jazz can kind of discover him. That's what Casey suggested, and I think it's a good plan. I'll just play it by ear from there," Kat said as Blaine pulled into her driveway.

"Where's Jazz now?" Blaine asked.

"She's probably on her dog bed in my bedroom. That's usually where she stays when I'm gone." Kat got out of the car and opened the back door for Rudy.

"Is your bedroom in the front or the back of the house?"

"It's in the back of the house, so Jazz won't be able to see Rudy get out of the car." She picked up his leash. "Come on, Rudy. Time to acclimate yourself to the back yard and get ready to meet Jazz." She opened the gate to the back yard and let him off leash. "Go ahead and explore, boy. You might think about assuring me that you're housebroken while you're at it." She came back through the gate and said, "Okay, he's in the back yard. Let's go in the house, and I'll let Jazz out. Think positive thoughts about what's coming next."

She walked into her bedroom and said, "I'm home, Jazz. It's time for you to go outside even though it's a lot warmer in here. Let's go."

Kat opened the sliding glass door and watched Jazz walk onto the porch and down the steps to the grass in the back yard. She stopped, sniffed the air, and then turned to where Rudy was standing at the rear of the yard. Kat's heart stood still as she waited for either dog to make a move. She turned around, so she wasn't looking at the yard or the dogs.

"Blaine, I can't stand this. What if Rudy hurts her? He outweighs her by more ten to one. I've read that Rottweilers have the most powerful jaws of all the different breeds of dogs. What if he puts Jazz's head in his mouth?"

"You can relax, Kat. I think you just got a free pass. Rudy is lying down while he lets Jazz sniff him. He just stood up and now he's sniffing her. All seems to be fine. Now they're running back and forth along the back fence, although Jazz has to take about five steps for every one Rudy takes. I think you could bring them in. Looks like they're going to get along with each other just fine."

Kat opened the door and called to the dogs. "Jazz, Rudy, come." The two polar opposites ran to the door, one small and white, the other large and black. It was truly a study in contrasts. Jazz ran over to where her toys were stored in a large basket at the far end of the family room. She looked back at Rudy as if to say, "Here's where my toys are. Want one?" He ambled over, pushed them around, and finally picked up a ball. A moment later he took it to Blaine.

"So you want to play ball, do you? Don't think Kat would appreciate it if we played in the house. I've still got my coat on, so let's go outside." The two of them walked over to the door with Jazz following. For the next fifteen minutes Blaine threw the ball in different directions, so both dogs had a chance to catch it. When they finally came back in the house, Rudy went to sleep on the dog bed Blaine had put down for him. Jazz sniffed it a few times and decided maybe it would be okay to have a big warm dog to sleep next to, and so she did.

Kat felt the knot in her stomach unwind. "Blaine I didn't realize how nervous I was about all of this," she said as her phone began to ring. "Excuse me, I better answer that." She looked at the screen and saw that it was Nick. "It's your brother."

"Nick, you'll be happy to know that I'm looking at a beautiful Rottweiler named Rudy who's sound asleep on his bed in my family room and my little Westie is asleep right next to him."

"That's just great," Nick said. "With him there my brother and I don't have to worry about you. From what Casey told me, Rudy can handle about any situation. I think you'll be very happy you got him."

"Blaine went to the kennel with me, and helped me introduce the two dogs. I really liked Casey, and his children are adorable. I promised his oldest boy, Stefan, that he could visit Rudy and have a play day with him. I think that helped with the separation. Evidently Rudy was his favorite dog."

"Casey's mentioned before that it's always hard on his wife and the children when one of the dogs leaves and yet, I think having a guard dog that's used to a family environment is an asset. Casey is very good at what he does."

"I'm not surprised. What did you find out about Tiffany and

where did you end up?" Kat asked.

"Kansas City."

Kat interrupted him. "You followed her to Kansas City? Where are you now?"

"I'm at the office. I didn't have a chance to tell you a few things I found out about her. The icing on the cake happened today. Why don't you sit down, if you're not already doing so? This is going to take a little time."

"Excuse me for just a moment." She put her hand over the phone and said, "Blaine, Nick said this is going to take a little while. If you want to stay, I'd love to fix you dinner."

"Tell you what, Kat. Talk to Nick and spend a little time getting to know Rudy. I'll go back to my office and work for a couple of hours. Would it be okay with you if I come back about 7:00 for dinner?"

"Perfect." She waved goodbye to him and said, "Sorry, Nick. Blaine was here, and I was just saying goodbye to him."

"No problem. Okay, here's the deal. Tiffany Conners met her husband in Kansas City when she was working as a pole dancer in a gentlemen's strip club that Lester used to go to whenever he was in Kansas City. Tiffany comes from a small town in southern Kansas and was a beauty queen in high school. From what I found out she really believed she could make it to Los Angeles or New York and be a movie or stage star, but she decided she needed to have a nose job and breast implants before she went. There weren't any plastic surgeons in her small town."

"A pole dancer? Wow! I'm not surprised about the plastic surgery. I always thought she looked a little too firm to be natural."

"Well, from what I found out she didn't stop there. She had her lips done and everything else she could afford. The problem was in order to afford all that she had to earn more money than she could make as a stripper. She began seeing men in her apartment for limited amounts of time, if you know what I mean."

"I have a pretty good idea what you're talking about. Sounds like something out of a novel."

"I agree, but Tiffany was smart. She realized at some point in time she was past the age where she could ever make it big in the movies or on stage. Lester had fallen in love with her, but he had no idea she was seeing men on the side. According to some people we talked to at the strip club, she told him she was very religious and felt horrible about her job, but when she'd left her hometown, she couldn't find a job, and she was almost starving. She revealed to him she'd gone to the manager of the apartment building where she lived and told him she didn't have enough money to pay her rent. He said he had a friend who owned a strip club and could probably hire her. From what her co-workers said, she seemed to thoroughly enjoy her work."

"Wow! You found out a lot in a short period of time, but I don't see what any of that has to do with me or why she'd be so upset about my book."

"I'm getting to that. She's been married to Lester Conners for five years now. Evidently she tried to adjust to the country club life and living in a sleepy university town, but she missed the excitement of the sex industry. From what I found out she had actually been in a couple of porn movies. A few months ago she contacted the producer she'd previously worked with, and that's where she went today. She spent several hours acting in a porn movie. When she read the copy of your book manuscript, I'm sure she became frightened that people would put two and two together and think the woman in your book who acts in porn movies was her. From what we could find out, her husband has no idea she's involved in any of this."

"I knew nothing about her. It was just something I made up and put in my book, but I can certainly see where she'd feel threatened. What do you think I should do?"

"For now, nothing. I'm concerned that if she was the one who murdered Nancy, there's a good chance she'll try to get rid of you too, so the story you wrote would never be published."

"I'm looking at a big black dog who will make sure nothing is going to happen to me, but remember, Barbara's the one who gave her the manuscript. I wonder if Barbara could be targeted by her."

"I don't know. I'm simply the messenger. You're the client, and you'll have to decide what to do about it."

"Let me think about it. Uhh, Rudy just stood up and walked over to the door. Maybe he wants to go outside. Can I call you back in a few minutes?"

"Sure. I'm going to be here for a while. You're not our only client. I need to check on a few things."

CHAPTER SIXTEEN

Kat walked over to where Rudy was standing by the door. When she opened it, a gust of cold wind entered the house, and she decided the weatherman had been right about a snowstorm coming soon. Winter darkness had descended, and the sky was black, giving the outdoors an eerie feeling. She was glad she'd brought Rudy home. Jazz followed him out the door, and a few minutes later she heard a scratch on the door. As soon as she opened it the two dogs raced in the house, happy to be in a warm place.

Better feed them, she thought. *Don't know how Rudy acts when he's hungry, but as big as he is and with that huge mouth of his, I don't think I want to find out if he bites the hand that feeds him. I've heard some dogs do that because they're in such a hurry to get their food.*

She wasn't sure how Rudy or Jazz would respond if she fed them in the same room, so she put Jazz in the laundry room and let Rudy eat in the kitchen. She set his dish in front of him, not sure what his reaction would be. He licked her hand and delicately took a bite of the dog food, looking up at Kat as if to reassure her she didn't need to worry. Luckily for her, he was a gentleman when he ate. When he was finished she let Jazz out of the laundry room, and the two dogs roamed through the house, going from one room to another.

They look like Mutt and Jeff. If this wasn't such a serious situation, I'd be amused, but I'm just fine with Rudy checking out the rooms. At least that's what he seems to be doing. Wonder if that was part of his training.

She picked up the phone and pressed in Nick's number. A moment later she heard his warm voice saying, "Well, how did he do?"

"Quite well. He's obviously housebroken, and I also fed him. He was as gentle as could be. It was almost as if he was trying to tell me not to worry about his strength, that he'd use it only if he needed to."

"Sounds like he's everything Casey said he'd be. Kat, I had one of my people do a thorough check on Sally Lonsdale. Here's what we found out. She grew up in Cimarron, a small town not too far from here. Her father was a Baptist minister, and from what my researcher found out, a real fire and brimstone one. She was an only child, and although he was conservative in his role as a minister, he was the epitome of rigidity when it came to his daughter and her upbringing.

"In a lot of cases like that the child rebels and becomes wild. Not so in this case. He believed all men were sinners, and he didn't want his daughter despoiled by a sinner. He preached about the evils of sex in the media, and claimed it was the root of the problems with the younger generation. He would not allow television in his home and regularly picketed the library to protest about certain books he felt were inappropriate for a public library."

"That would seem to fit with what I know about her."

"There's some more. Her mother died of breast cancer at an early age, and even though Sally did get married, she's devoted to her father and spends a great deal of time with him. He's quite elderly, but still attends church and pickets the library from time to time. From what my researcher found out, Sally never had a chance to live the life most young people do. She's currently very active in the church, and that's how she met Carl Jennings. His wife, Nancy, wasn't as religious as her husband and often didn't attend church. Carl was there every Sunday and was just as active in church life as Sally. There was never anything romantic between them, just two people who shared a common cause - eliminating what they considered to be anything deemed sexually unsuitable.

"Sally is a certified public accountant and has a small tax practice. She lives very frugally, although her husband has a good job. She drives a fifteen-year-old car, and we saw nothing that would indicate they ever traveled, not even to Kansas City, which isn't that far away. She's a reader, but she gets her books at the library. About the only expense we noted was their membership in the country club, but that seems to be because her husband's hobby is golf."

"Nick, I don't have a feeling that she's a real threat."

"Well, yes and no. On the surface from what we found out, she has never acted in an aggressive manner, but she is rabid on the subject of sex, and we know that she read your manuscript. Sometimes people simply flip out and lose all sense of the difference between right and wrong.

"It's like a switch has been turned on in their brain, and they have a sudden impulse to take some sort of dramatic action. In this case that dramatic action might very well have led her to commit murder. Although I don't think that's what happened, I won't rule it out. I'm just glad you have Rudy with you."

"So am I. Now what?" Kat asked.

"I have someone following her and observing if there's any unusual activity on her part. I'm also having more research done on Tiffany Connors. Lastly, I have someone following Carl as well. Since those are the three suspects so far in this case, that should take care of them. Of course, there's always the chance that whoever murdered Nancy is not one of those three. I should know more tomorrow morning. I'll call you then if I find out anything."

"Thanks, Nick. I'm so glad Blaine suggested you, and I'm so glad you suggested Rudy. I don't think I really appreciated how nervous I was last night. With him here, I'm sure I'll get a good night's sleep tonight. Talk to you in the morning. I've invited your brother for dinner, so I probably better start fixing it. We certainly don't want the new district attorney starving. Who knows what kind of bad decisions he could make? Thanks again for your help."

CHAPTER SEVENTEEN

"Were you able to get anything done when you went back to the office?" Kat asked as she opened the door for Blaine.

"I was able to tie up a few loose ends, so it was a productive ninety minutes. And you," he said as he took off his coat, "did Nick tell you anything of interest?"

"Lots. Come on in the kitchen, and I'll tell you all about it while I put the finishing touches on dinner. Would you like a glass of wine or a drink?"

"Definitely. Whatever you have would be fine. Thanks," he said as he sat down at the kitchen table. She poured two glasses of wine and handed one to him. He took a sip and said, "This is wonderful. What is it?"

"It's a Stag's Leap cabernet sauvignon. My husband was a wine connoisseur and felt that if a person was going to drink wine, it should only be good wine. It was pretty much a rule in our house and one which I still ascribe to, and it does make for enjoyable meals."

"What are you making us for dinner?"

"It's one of my favorites, but it takes a little doing, so I never bother just for myself. It's called manicotti, which is a large tubular type of pasta that's stuffed with chicken and Italian sausage and then covered with marinara sauce and mozzarella cheese. I hope you enjoy it. I thought I'd make a green salad and some toasted garlic bread to go with it. Sound okay to you?"

"Sounds a whole lot better than okay. I'm of the camp that believes good eating should be the 11th Commandment, and from what I'm hearing, I think this is a meal I'm definitely going to enjoy."

"Hope you feel that way after you're finished."

"Where's Rudy?"

"He looked out the window when he heard your car pull up. He must have recognized you, because he saw you get out, and then he went upstairs along with Jazz. If he didn't recognize you this guard dog thing might be a myth."

"I don't think so. Now, tell me what Nick had to say."

She took a sip of her wine and began to relate what Nick had told her about Tiffany, Carl, and Sally. When she was finished he sat quietly for a moment, twisting the stem of his wine glass. "Kat, you know I'm a lawyer, and I've worked on a lot of criminal cases over the years. Quite honestly any one of those three people could have killed Nancy, but the thing I always start with is who has the most to gain from the person being murdered."

"That's an interesting place to start. I don't see Sally having anything to gain other than a book that she thought shouldn't be published wouldn't be. I find it difficult to believe that so small of a motive could result in murder," Kat said.

"I agree, but I've also seen what I would consider second tier suspects wind up being the killer. I wouldn't rule her out, but I agree with you, she doesn't strike me as being the murderer."

Kat furrowed her brow as if trying to catch a fleeting thought. "This is really off the wall, Blaine, but what if her father found out about the book? As incensed as she seemed to be from what Bev overheard at the salon, and as much time as she seems to spend with him, maybe she told him about it. I wonder if he'd be capable of murder. I don't know if he's even physically healthy enough to do something like that, although Nick did say he still picketed the library and occasionally gave a sermon."

"Only one way to find out," he said, pulling his phone out of his pocket and punching a number in. "Hey, Nick, I'm here with Kat, and we have a question for you. What are the chances that Sally's father is the murderer? From what you told Kat he would certainly see the book as the devil's dealings. What we'd like to know is if he's physically capable of committing murder."

"Off the top of my head, I don't think so, but let me do a little research. It's actually a pretty good thought. I'll get back to Kat later tonight or in the morning," Nick said.

"Okay, Kat, that takes care of Sally and her father. Carl's a wild card to me. On one hand he seemed to love his wife, but on the other hand he strongly disapproved, maybe even more than strongly, of Nancy editing your books. Is that motive enough to kill her? And wouldn't he know that he and his daughter would probably become estranged if he committed the murder?"

Blaine continued, "On the other hand, he might consider his wife dirty because she edited your books, and if he got rid of her, he would be doing something to help cleanse the world of the filth he thinks is overtaking it. I know that's a bit of a stretch, but it could cause him to become a prime suspect. What bothers me is his relationship with his daughter. Is his hatred of books such as yours deep enough that he would risk losing his daughter?"

"I don't know," Kat responded. "From what Lacie said, Nicole doesn't want anything to do with her father. Evidently he and Nancy had words over this subject before, and Nicole thought he was out of line. She was very close to her mother and is devastated over her death."

"I know you mentioned Lacie asked you if Nicole could spend the holidays here. You know that's not going to sit well with Carl. I'm wondering if you could talk to him about it. Maybe you could set up a meeting and you, Carl, and Nicole could talk about the situation in a rational manner. I have a feeling if he just finds out she's going to spend the holidays here in your home, he not only is not going to be happy, he may want to take it out on you."

"Let me think about that, but it does sound like a pretty good idea. I called Lacie, and she's coming over after dinner tonight to meet Rudy. Why don't you stay, and we can talk about it then?"

"I'd be happy to. Now let's get to Tiffany. What more, if anything, is Nick going to do about her?"

"I don't know. He said he'd probably have something more for me in the morning. What's your thinking about her?"

"Well, I started out this conversation by saying to look at who has the most to gain by killing Nancy. Although, I consider Carl and Sally to be very viable suspects, I'd have to say that Tiffany is at the top of my list. If your book is published, evidently she's afraid that people will think she's the person in the book who's having an affair and working in the porn film industry. It's not much of a stretch for her to be concerned her husband will find out and divorce her. Without him she's got nothing, and she's put on a few years since she was working as a dancer at a strip joint in Kansas City and having meetings with strange men with money in her apartment. She might feel that with Nancy dead, the book would never be published, but there's always the chance you could write another one. If it is her, your life could definitely be in danger."

Kat was quiet and then said, "Blaine, I'm not the only one whose life could be in jeopardy. Remember, Barbara, the hostess at the country club, was the one who found the manuscript under the table where Nancy ate lunch. Barbara's the one who copied the manuscript, and Tiffany may wonder if Barbara read it. If so, she might feel that Barbara would have to be eliminated. Granted, all of this is a stretch, but it's still a possibility, and quite frankly, a possibility I don't like."

"This is exactly why I'm glad you have Rudy. Kat, I want to change the subject, but before I do I have to tell you that manicotti smells delicious."

"Good, hold the thought because it's time to eat. I set the table in the dining room. I'm a big candle person, so if you'd light them for me, I'll put dinner on the table."

Just as they were finishing eating, they heard Rudy growl and start barking. A moment later there was a knock on the door. Rudy stood next to Kat as she asked, "Who's there?"

"Mom, it's me." Kat opened the door and let Lacie in. "When I heard that bark, there was no way I was walking in and introducing myself to Rudy. I'll let you do that." She looked over her mother's shoulder and said, "Blaine, is that a gun you're putting in your pocket?"

Kat whirled around and looked at him. "What is that all about?"

Blaine spread his hands out in a 'You Caught Me' gesture and said, "Just didn't want you to be surprised. Thought I'd back up Rudy if he needed it."

"Mom, you certainly have your protectors. Why don't you introduce me to Rudy, so I feel safe enough to walk in the other room? Gotta tell you, that is one big wicked looking dog."

"Rudy, meet Lacie. She's a friend and my daughter. She's safe, Rudy, safe." She looked from Blaine to Lacie and said, "That's the word I'm supposed to use to tell Rudy that someone is all right and not to be thought of as a potential enemy."

Lacie put her hand on the big dog's head and petted him. "Hi, Rudy. Let's be friends. You take care of Mom. Okay?" The big dog continued to stand next to where Kat was as if he understood what Lacie had just said.

"Mom, if you don't want him, I'll take him."

"Down the road, maybe. Don't see the housemother of the Pi Phi sorority house being too thrilled with having a hundred-twenty-pound-dog living in the house, and probably a number of the girls there are afraid of dogs. We just finished dinner, and if you don't mind I'd like to talk to you about Nicole."

CHAPTER EIGHTEEN

"Blaine and I were just getting ready to have dessert. I made some brownies, and even though I'm sure snow is imminent and it's cold out, I thought they'd go well with vanilla ice cream. Would you like to join us?" Kat asked.

"Mom, you know I've never met a brownie I didn't like, and if you made those killer fudgy brownies that you know I'm crazy about, I'll take two, thank you very much," Lacie said, laughing as she pulled a chair out from the dining room table. No one said anything for a few minutes as the three of them enjoyed the brownies and ice cream.

"I have to agree with Lacie, Kat. I'll take another one. These are the best brownies I've ever had, and they're one of my favorite indulgences," Blaine said.

"Good, glad you like them." After she'd given Blaine seconds, Kat turned to Lacie and asked, "How's Nicole doing today?"

"Better, but I'm not sure you ever get over having your mother murdered. She asked me again if she could stay with me over the Christmas break. I told her I was seeing you tonight, and I'd ask you what your decision was."

"Lacie, I'm really uncomfortable about this for a number of

reasons. First and foremost, I don't want to get in the middle of a disagreement between Nicole and Carl. I really think they need to work out their differences. In my opinion, with Nancy gone, they should be there for each other. I know Nicole's old enough to be considered an adult, but I kind of feel there's a moral issue here. I don't want Carl thinking I'm stepping in and trying to become a mother to Nicole, particularly after the things he said to me when I found Nancy's body."

"You never told me about that. What did he say?"

Blaine answered for her. "I think it could be summed up by saying he thought your mother was a terrible influence on Nancy and an evil person. He more or less blamed your mother for her death."

"That's ridiculous. Why would anyone think that?"

"I have no idea," Blaine responded. "Evidently he was pretty brainwashed by his father regarding anything that has to do with sex. Kat found out that Carl's mother left his father and him when Carl was quite young, and after she left she lived with a number of different men. We think Carl was afraid Nancy might do the same."

"In a twisted way, I guess that makes some sense," Lacie said. "Nicole's never mentioned it to me. The only thing she's told me is that her father wouldn't let her date when she lived at home, and she got a late start by having her first date in college. Judging by the number of nights she's out on dates now, I think she's making up for it." She stopped and realized how that might be interpreted.

"Mom, I know what you're thinking, but you're wrong. In her own way, Nicole is very conservative. She loves going out on dates and the attention she's getting, but that's it. I'd be willing to bet everything I have, which I know isn't much, that she's still a virgin, and I sure can't say that about the majority of my sorority sisters."

"I think you've given me enough information about Nicole and that topic. Let's get back to Carl. There's a second reason I'm a little concerned about having Nicole stay here. If Carl is the murderer, I'm sorry Lacie, but he is considered a suspect, anyway if he is, I could be his next target and getting between him and Nicole would only give him a further reason to do something to me."

"Oh, wow! I can see why you're having trouble with having her spend the Christmas holidays here. I'm sorry to ask this, Mom, but would you meet with Nicole? I know she's going to be very hurt if you turn her down, but maybe if you explained this to her it would help. How about if I give her a call, and you two set up a meeting? I don't think I even need to be there. Maybe you'll feel differently if you talk to her in person, and if you decide she can't stay here, at least she'll hear it from you and not me. If I tell her, there's a good chance she'll get mad at me, and I don't want to lose her as a friend. Matter of fact, right now she needs all the friends she can get."

"Yes, I agree. I probably do need to talk to her. Go ahead and call her."

*****

"Hi, Nicole it's Lacie. I'm at Mom's house. She was wondering if the two of you could get together in the next couple of days and talk about you spending the holidays with us."

"Sure, Lacie," Nicole responded. "I'm going over to my house tomorrow about 2:00 to pick up a dress I need to wear to a fraternity party this weekend. I'm hoping it will take my mind off of everything that's happened. Would that work for her?"

"I don't know, let me ask her." Lacie turned to Kat and said, "Mom, Nicole says she could meet you at her house at 2:00 tomorrow. Okay with you?"

"Yes, that would be fine. I have a couple of other things I need to do in the morning, so tomorrow afternoon will work for me," Kat said.

"Nicole, Mom says that's fine."

"Tell her to go in the house through the back door if my car isn't parked behind the house," Nicole said. "She can park in the alley behind the house. I drive a little red car, and she won't be able to miss it. If she doesn't see it, there's a key under the door mat. It looks like it's going to be snowing tomorrow, so I don't want her waiting outside in the cold for me. She's probably gone in the house that way before. Mom, Dad, and I rarely use the front door. It's more for strangers. Please tell her I hope she'll say yes about letting me stay with you."

"I will. How would you like to have a brownie? Mom just made a killer batch, and I'm leaving now for the sorority house. Sound good? I learned from mom that chocolate makes everything seem better."

"She's right. I think the only thing I've eaten today is the coffee cake you brought me earlier. That sounds great. It's been a pretty stressful day. I think my dad must have called me twenty times. I don't want to see him or talk to him. Actually, I'd love it if you could snag two brownies from her. That's the only bright thing that's happened to me today."

"Shouldn't be a problem. See you in a few minutes," Lacie said as she ended the call. She turned to Kat. "You're to meet her at her house at 2:00 tomorrow. Would you like me to be there?"

"No," Kat said. "I think this should be between Nicole and me, and I really don't know what I'm going to say. I just hope Carl doesn't show up."

What Kat didn't know was that Carl showing up would save hers and Nicole's lives, with a little help from Rudy.

CHAPTER NINETEEN

"Kat, thanks again for dinner. That manicotti dish was fabulous. Chicken, pasta, gooey cheese, and marina sauce. I loved it. Seriously, that was one of the best things I've had in a long time. I know you're impressed with the new chef at the country club, but trust me, he could take some lessons from you.

"I'm glad you had a chance to introduce Rudy to Lacie, and he approved of her. I'll be curious how your meeting goes with Nicole tomorrow. Would you give me a call after you talk to her?" He patted Rudy on his head and put on his heavy winter coat. "Besides Nicole, what else is on your agenda for tomorrow?"

"I'm going to write in the morning. With everything that's happened lately, I'm getting behind, and I need to find a new editor. I've come to learn that my eyes just don't pick up my mistakes. I guess it's because I see what's in my mind rather than what's missing on the printed page. That's why I need another set of eyes on my work. I'm thinking about asking Bev. Do you think Jim would have any objections?"

"From the rough type of language he uses on the golf course, I think he'd be the last person to complain if his wife edited your books. Why are you thinking of using her rather than getting a professional editor?"

"What I need from an editor is someone to point out my mistakes, like when I use the wrong character's name, or there's an inconsistency in a time line. Bev was an English Literature major when she was in college, and I know she reads several books a week. She was very interested in my books when she heard I was writing under a pen name, and she even ordered a couple from Amazon. She lives near me, she's very honest, and I trust her judgment. For all of those reasons I think she'd be able to do a good job for me."

"Given what you've told me, I think that could certainly take care of your editing problems. Would you pay her?"

"Absolutely," Kat said. "I couldn't ask her to do this as a favor to me. Plus, if she's getting paid she's going to be a lot more diligent, don't you think?"

"Yes," Blaine said. "I've always thought she was one of the smartest people I've ever met, and I think she'd make a great editor. Uh-oh," he said, looking out the window. "The predicted snow has arrived. I don't know how much we'll get, but from the way the wind is blowing, we may be in for a real storm. Be careful when you drive tomorrow.

"One last thing, and then I'll get out of your hair. When you go to meet Nicole tomorrow, would you please take Rudy with you? I'm probably being overly cautious, but I'm worried about you being at Carl's house, so please also put your gun in your purse. I see your raised eyebrows, Kat, but I've been in too many courtrooms and seen too many criminals over the years, so I always err on the side of caution, and I definitely think this is one time you should too. Trust me, strange things happen."

"All right. If it will make you feel better, I'll take Rudy with me. I'm also going to stop by the club and talk to Barbara. If Nancy's death was caused because of my manuscript, as I mentioned before, whoever did it has to wonder if Barbara made a copy for herself along with the copies she made for Sally and Tiffany."

He put his arms around her and gently kissed her. "Kat, I really don't want anything to happen to you. I like being with you. It feels right to me."

"I feel the same way, Blaine. I think you better go now, because if you don't, I might ask you to stay, and we both might regret it."

He opened the door and grinned at her. "Believe me when I tell you that is not something I'd regret." He turned and walked down the steps to his car as she closed the door after him.

A few minutes later she said, "Rudy, Jazz. Time to go outside for the last time tonight. I don't want to have to get up in the middle of the night, so make this visit count." She turned on the security lights in the back yard and let the two dogs out. She could barely see Jazz against the white snow which had started to blanket the back yard, but there was no missing the big black Rottweiler. From the way he was running and jumping in the snow, she wondered if he remembered what snow was like from when he was a puppy.

I just hope they'll be as willing to go out in the snow tomorrow. From the looks of it, it's here to stay for a while, and it looks like it's going to be pretty deep by morning.

She let the dogs back in the house, turned off the lights, and walked down the hall, looking forward to a good night's sleep now that she had a guard dog to stand watch and protect her.

CHAPTER TWENTY

The next morning when Kat woke up she looked outside at what appeared to be at least eight inches of fresh snow. It was still snowing heavily and from the looks of the stormy sky, it wasn't going to let up anytime soon. Refreshed from a good night's sleep, she went down the hall to the kitchen to make coffee and let the dogs out. She saw that the snow had been cleared from her driveway and sidewalk and she said a silent thank you to the person the homeowner's association had hired last year to do just that.

She dressed and went into her office, sat down at her computer, and started writing. It took a while for her to get back in the swing of it after everything that had recently happened, but when her phone rang two hours later, she realized she'd been totally absorbed in what she was doing. She picked up the phone and saw that the call was from Nick.

"Good morning, Nick, how are you?"

"Glad to be finished shoveling snow. It was my wife's turn to carpool our daughter and her friends to school, so I had to get it done before she left. I wanted you to know about something interesting I found out last night. I don't think I told you that when I was tailing Tiffany Conners she left the porn studio and drove to an upscale condominium building in the Country Club Plaza area of Kansas City. I wanted to dig a little deeper and see what I could find out about the man who was about Tiffany's age and walked out of the studio with her. They got in separate cars and later met at the condo.

"I was able to find out who he is. He's a well-known porn star, and a source of mine told me Tiffany's been having an affair with him since she went back to acting in porn movies. Evidently she films weekly, and when she's finished, she always meets him at his condo. He's married and get this, his wife is the owner of the porn studio. My source said his wife doesn't have any idea that he and Tiffany are having an affair."

"Wow! What do you make of all that?" Kat asked.

"Tiffany certainly would have a motive for not wanting your book to be published. From what you've told me one of the characters in your book belongs to a country club, is younger than her husband, and is having an affair. She certainly might have been afraid that when people read the book knowing that you wrote it and you belong to a country club, that someone would think it was her and might tell her husband.

"It looks like her lover isn't going to divorce his wife, at least that's what my source said. His wife is older and he's kind of her boy toy. She makes a lot of money from the porn studio, and he's not about to walk away from all that money in order to be with Tiffany. Evidently this isn't the first woman he's had an affair with. My source said that when his wife finds out, he promises to be faithful and that it will never happen again. She takes him back every time, and then the cycle starts all over again. Tiffany must know he's not going to marry her, and if her husband left her, which he probably would, she'd have nowhere to go, and her life would be ruined. In other words, your book threatened to completely upend her life."

"Yes, I can see where she would think that. And who knows? I may have subconsciously drawn that character from Tiffany, although I certainly had no factual basis to believe she was having an affair, and quite frankly, I'm not sure I ever even thought about it. I don't know what to do with this information. Nick, what do you think?"

"In cases like this, I usually advise that you don't do anything for the time being. Something will probably come to a head sooner or later and you can make a decision then."

"Thanks, Nick, that's good advice. Anything else?"

"Not at the moment. I'm going to be working on a couple of other cases today, but if you think of something, give me a call. There's not much more I can do with your case right now."

"You've done an excellent job in a very short period of time. I'll see what the next couple of days bring, and then I'll get back to you."

"Okay. Be careful if you have to go out today. My wife said the streets are a mess. It's the first bad snow storm of the year, and a lot of people forget what it's like to drive on snow and ice."

"Thanks. I do have to go out, but I'll be careful. Talk to you later."

Kat looked at her watch and decided she had enough time to give Bev a call before she left to see Barbara at the country club. A few moments later she heard Bev's voice. "Hi, Kat, what's up with you on this snowy day? I'm going to make a big fire in a few minutes and do nothing but read a book while I'm sitting in front of it keeping warm."

"Sounds wonderful. Wish I could join you," Kat said. "Actually that's kind of why I'm calling. Remember how we talked about my writing at lunch the other day and that Nancy was my editor? As you know she was murdered. Some people think it might have been tied to my book, and that I should be very careful. I got a big protective Rottweiler guard dog yesterday, so actually I feel pretty safe with him around. Bev, I know you're an avid reader and that you majored in English Literature in college. Have you ever done any editing?"

"No, but it's something I've always been interested in. Why?"

"I need to find an editor and rather than look for one on the Internet or ask other authors who they use, I was wondering if you'd be interested in being my editor. I don't know if you've had a chance to read the books of mine that you ordered, but when you do, I'd like you to see if they're the type you think you might enjoy editing."

She was interrupted by Bev. "Kat, I've already read them, and I love them. I can't think of anything I'd rather do than be your editor. When do you want me to start?"

"That's great. I'd like you to start as soon as possible. I'd hoped to get The Country Club Cover-Up ready for publication in a couple of days, but with Nancy's death, I never got her editing notes. Tell you what. I'll email you a copy of the manuscript. You can read it and make notes. If you spot typos or verb tense errors, you can edit those right on the copy. If it's something to do with a character or the plot, I'd prefer those to be noted separately. By the way, this is a job, and I'll pay you for doing it. Based on what Nancy's husband thought of the type of books I write, I feel I have to ask if editing this genre would be a problem for Jim. Given everything that's happened, I certainly wouldn't want you to do it if he objected to it."

"Not in the least, and don't give that a second thought. He's one of the most liberal people I know. He could care less what I read as long as I enjoy it. I'd be willing to bet there are a lot of people in this town who read your books even if they don't admit it. You don't ever need to feel guilty about them. Look at it this way. No one is forcing anyone to buy a certain book. Kat, you're a very good writer. I became thoroughly engaged in each of your books that I read because the dialogue, the characters, and the plots were so good. Don't ever apologize for what you write."

"Thanks, Bev. I really appreciate hearing that. I hate to admit it, but during the last couple of days I've been having second thoughts about the types of books I've been writing."

"Well, forget it. When can I expect to get that manuscript from you?"

"I'll get it off to you right now, and I'm so glad you agreed to do this. Thank you so much."

"You don't need to thank me," Bev said, "I'm the one who should be thanking you for thinking of me. I can't wait to get started. I might even have something for you as early as tomorrow. Talk to you later."

CHAPTER TWENTY-ONE

Kat drove into the parking lot of the country club at 1:15 and wondered if they were closed because of the snow storm, since the parking lot was almost empty. "Rudy, there's no need for you to come with me. I'll be perfectly safe at the club." She opened the door of her car and gasped as a frigid blast of freezing wind almost blew her over. She walked up the steps, holding tightly onto the railing, afraid that beneath the snow that covered the steps was a sheet of ice. The snow was coming down so hard it was almost blinding her. She opened the door and stepped inside, grateful for the warmth.

She saw Barbara standing at the hostess stand, but there was no one else in the dining room. Kat walked over to her and said, "Hi, Barbara. I guess I'm the only one stupid enough to brave the storm."

"I wouldn't say you were stupid, but it looks like we're going to remain empty all day. The manager just told me I could leave at 2:00 this afternoon if no one comes in. I'm surprised you ventured out for lunch today."

"Barbara, I'm not here for lunch. I want to talk to you. It looks like I picked a good day for it since no one is here."

"Sure. We can sit at a table, if you'd like. I usually stand during the entire time we're open for lunch, so I'm always ready to sit down." She led Kat to a table that was near the hostess stand and said, "We can sit here. If anyone comes in, I'll be able to see them, but I don't think that's going to happen. What did you want to talk to me about?"

"We talked earlier this week about the manuscript of mine that fell out of Nancy's tote bag and how you made two copies and gave one to Tiffany Conners and one to Sally Lonsdale. You also said you had given the original to Carl Jennings, Nancy's husband. Correct?"

"Yes. That's what I told you."

"Did you keep a copy for yourself?"

Barbara avoided eye contact with Kat and looked down at her hands as she began twisting them, clearly agitated. She cleared her throat, obviously reluctant to answer Kat's question. Finally, she looked up at Kat and said, "Yes." Then she began to speak rapidly. "I think I told you my husband lost his job, and money's real tight for us right now. I love to read, and I haven't been able to afford any books since he's been out of work. I figured if I made an extra copy of the manuscript for myself, I'd get to read your book for free and no one would know. I took the extra copy of the manuscript home and read it. Mrs. Denham, I didn't give it to anyone else, it was just for me."

"I understand," Kat said. "Being a reader, if it was me I might have done the same thing. Here's what's worrying me. Some people think Nancy was murdered because she was my editor, and whoever did it didn't want to see my book published. If that's true, there's a strong possibility that my life might be in danger. As a matter of fact, just yesterday I got a large Rottweiler guard dog who's with me all the time, at least everywhere but places I know are safe for me, like here. I left him in my car."

"When I was growing up, I had a Rottweiler dog," Barbara said. "They're a wonderful breed. I remember how protective my dog was about me. Once when I was riding my bike a boy rode by me and kicked my bike. My dog grabbed the boy's pant leg with his teeth and caused him to fall off of his bike and scrape his leg. His father demanded that we get rid of the dog, or he'd go to the police and file a complaint. My parents decided they had to get rid of the dog. All of us were so sad. The poor dog couldn't help it, because he was just doing what he was hardwired to do."

"That's a sad childhood memory. I hope your parents found a good home for him."

"They did. They put an ad in the paper, and as soon as it came out a farmer in a small town not too far from here called and said the dog would be perfect for him. He had a large fenced yard, but since there weren't any houses nearby, he always worried something might happen to his wife and children when he was off working in the fields. He wanted to get a guard dog and asked if he could bring his family to meet the dog. They came that very day and took him home with them. I'm sure he had a very good life."

"I'm glad. I'll have to remember not to ride a bike when Rudy's with me," Kat said smiling. "Barbara, here's what I'm concerned about. If Nancy was murdered because of my book and someone wants to make sure it's never published, and if they find out you have a copy, you could be in danger."

Barbara's eyes grew wide as she comprehended what Kat was saying. "Do you really think someone would try to hurt me because I have a copy of the manuscript?"

"I don't know, but I wanted you to be aware of the possibility in case anything out of the ordinary occurs. Have you had any strange calls or is there anything else you can think of that might be suspicious?"

Barbara was quiet for a moment and then she said, "The only thing that's a little strange is that I got a call from Tiffany Conners yesterday. She asked me if I'd made any extra copies of the manuscript. I lied and said no. I didn't want her to think I'd do something like that. Then she asked me if I had returned the original manuscript to Nancy. I told her I hadn't given it to Nancy, but instead I'd given it to her husband, so he could give it to Nancy. At the time I wondered why she'd want to know."

"So do I. Do you know much about her?"

Barbara involuntarily looked around to see if anyone could hear her, but no one except the two of them was in the empty room. The club was eerily silent. "I shouldn't say this, but I don't think she's as much in love with her husband as she pretends to be when she's with him."

"What makes you say that?"

"Well," Barbara said. "It's nothing she's said, but I've noticed she smiles a lot at other men when her husband's playing golf, and she's waiting for him in the bar. A couple of the men have bought her drinks and talked to her. As soon as she sees her husband she leaves them and goes to another table, like she's been sitting there alone just waiting for him to finish his round of golf. She always runs up to him and kisses him. It's obvious he's crazy in love with her."

"What else have you heard?" Kat asked.

Barbara seemed very uncomfortable and said, "I've probably talked too much as it is."

"If there's something else about her you think I should know, please tell me. I'm trying to find out who murdered Nancy, and although I'm not at liberty to tell you everything I know, I can tell you that Tiffany is a person of interest. Please, Barbara, both of our lives could possibly be in jeopardy."

"Well, you didn't hear this from me. Johnny, one of the bartenders, was clearing the table next to where Tiffany and Pete Hammond were sitting. You know, he's the club's tennis pro. Anyway, Johnny heard Pete tell her he'd open his garage door, and she could drive in when she went to his house the next day. Johnny was pretty sure what that meant."

"What did he think it meant?"

"Probably the same thing you're thinking. It sure seemed like Tiffany was going to visit Pete, and I don't think it was for a tennis lesson."

"Hmmm. If that's true, do you think her husband has any idea about what's going on?"

"Not from the way he treats her. I've never understood how these older men believe that their young arm candy wife is really in love with them. Why can't they see that the women are just in it for their money? It's pretty obvious to everybody else."

"I don't know, but maybe men like that have blinders on when it comes to age and money. Or maybe they feel it's a fair trade. They get a beautiful younger woman on their arm, and in return they share their money with their new young wife. Come to think of it, it actually is a fair trade. Each one of them is getting something. In a strange way it's kind of like a business deal. Barbara, I've got to meet someone at 2:00, and it may take me longer than usual to get there with this storm, so I'm going to have to leave now as it's getting close to two o'clock. If you think of anything else or if you feel something is strange, please give me a call. Here's my cell phone number."

CHAPTER TWENTY-TWO

Kat drove through the snow-clogged empty streets of Lindsay to Nancy's house, pulling into the alley behind it as Nicole had instructed her to do. The strong wind had blown away the snow that had probably been in the alley earlier. She remembered teasing Nancy about painting the doors of the garage red. Nancy had responded that red doors were good luck, and if the front door of her house could be red, so could her garage doors. Kat smiled thinking about Nancy's comment that she was sure none of her family would ever have a traffic accident because of the doors being painted red. Kat drove her car to a space between the house and the garage, noticing that Nicole's little red car wasn't there yet.

"Rudy, sorry to do this to you, but you're going to have to go in with me. Oh dear, I remember something Nancy said about how Carl wanted a big dog, but they weren't sure whether Nicole was allergic to dogs. I have no idea if they ever had her tested, but think you better stay on the covered porch until I find out. I completely forgot about that when I let Jazz come in with me the day I discovered her body. Anyway, you'll be shielded from the snow and since the porch has glass sides, it shouldn't be too cold. Let's go."

Kat got out of her car, and Rudy followed her up the steps and onto the porch. She bent down and took the key from under the mat and opened the door. When she closed it behind her she thought she heard voices in another part of the house. The sounds were coming from Nancy's office. She walked toward it, and although she knew she'd heard the voice before, she couldn't quite place whose voice it was.

"I don't know why you came here today," the voice said. "I thought you college girls just partied all the time, but I can't let you live after finding me here. I've got the manuscript, and now I'm going to have to kill you just like I killed your mother."

Kat peeked around the corner of the door leading to the office and saw Nicole sitting in a chair. Tiffany Conners had a gun in her hand, and it was pointed at Nicole. As Kat tried to step back and away from the doorway she tripped over the throw rug in the hall and fell to her knees. Tiffany pointed the gun at her and shouted, "Stand up, Kat, and get in here, or I'll shoot you. I did a western type movie once, and I became a crack shot. If I shoot you, I won't have to waste a second shot to kill you."

Kat stood up and walked into the room, wishing she hadn't left Rudy on the porch and her purse with her gun in it in the car. *So much for vanity,* she thought, *I didn't want my new leather purse to get wet from the snow. Heck of a lot of good the gun does me when it's in the car and I'm in here.*

"Sit down in that chair next to Nicole. Guess I'll have to kill you, too," Tiffany said with a maniacal laugh. "You're the one who wrote the book. I've found the original manuscript, and I'm going to burn it. I burned my copy, and I told Sally Lonsdale that book should never be published, and I would be happy to burn it to make sure it wasn't. She agreed and gave her copy to me. With you dead, now it will never be published."

Kat didn't know what else to do but to try and keep Tiffany talking. It was a ploy she always used in her books when the heroine needed a little extra time to wiggle out of a tight spot, and it seemed like the only thing she could do now.

"Tiffany, I know you think that the character in my book, Chastity, is you, but I never based her on you. I'll make you a deal. If you let Nicole and me go, I promise that book will never be published. No one will ever think you're Chastity."

"How stupid do you think I am? I never got to be the wife of the town banker by being stupid. I may not have some fancy schmancy college degree, but I've got street smarts, and they're worth a whole lot more than some diploma." Just then, all three of them heard sounds coming from the back of the house.

"What was that?" Tiffany asked with a nervous look on her face.

"I have no idea," Kat answered.

"Be quiet," Tiffany said, cocking her head and swinging the barrel of the pistol towards the empty doorway.

CHAPTER TWENTY-THREE

Carl Jennings got in his car and began the drive home, noticing how empty the streets were because of the storm. He thought about his attempts to contact his daughter, Nicole, and how she'd refused to answer his calls.

It's bad enough Nancy's dead. Now it's as if my daughter's dead too. Nancy always told me I was too rigid with Nicole. I'm beginning to think she was right. Maybe I should see a shrink and get some help for what Nancy always called my "sex hang up." If I got some help, maybe Nicole and I could have a normal father-daughter relationship. Right now I feel like I don't have anything to live for. Nancy was my life, and when I found out she was editing Kat's books, I was sure she was going to leave me, just like Mom left Dad. I'm sorry Nicole heard us arguing about Sexy Cissy, but I loved Nancy so much I couldn't bear the thought of her leaving.

Carl drove into the alley behind his house and saw a strange car parked in the space between the house and the garage.

That's odd. No one is in the car. Wonder what's going on.

He turned off the engine and walked up the steps to the porch. Inside he saw a big Rottweiler dog patiently standing there as if someone had gone into the house and left him there. "Here, big guy," he said to the dog, carefully holding his hand out so the dog could sniff it. Rudy inspected Carl's hand and then licked it. In spite of the emotional pain Carl was in, he couldn't help but smile at the dog. "Okay guy, it's too cold for either one of us to be out here. It's my house, so come on in and let's see how you wound up out here on my back porch." The door knob easily turned in Carl's hand and he realized the door was unlocked. He yelled, "Hey, is anyone here?"

When no one answered, he walked down the hall followed by Rudy. A moment later he heard a woman's voice say, "We're in the office."

Carl took one step into the room that had been Nancy's office and said, "What..." At the same time Kat gave a hand and finger motion to Rudy that had been in the instruction papers that Casey had given her. Just as he had been trained to do in situations like this, Rudy leaped forward and his massive jaws clamped around one of Tiffany's legs as she cried out in pain, causing the gun she'd been holding to fall to the floor.

Carl ran over to where Nicole was. "Honey, are you all right? Did she hurt you? What's going on?"

"No, I'm fine, Daddy." She started crying, and he took her in his arms.

The moment the gun fell from Tiffany's hand, Kat jumped out of her chair and grabbed it. She pointed it at Tiffany and said, "You may be a crack shot, but so am I. Stay where you are, or I'll give Rudy the command to really do some damage to that plastic body of yours. Carl, Nicole, I'm calling the police chief. The danger is over. We're all going to be fine."

While they waited for the police chief, Carl said, "Kat, Nicole, why are the two of you here?"

Nicole spoke first and said, "I asked Kat's daughter if I could spend the holidays with them at their house, and we were meeting here today to talk about it. Dad, after everything's that happened, I didn't want to spend my Christmas break from school here. I know you probably don't understand, but since I've been away at college, I see things differently. I always thought there was something wrong with me for wanting to go out on dates and have fun. I've learned that all people my age feel that way. You don't understand that about me, so maybe it's better if we don't see that much of each other."

Carl answered by saying, "Since your mother died, and you haven't answered my phone calls, I've done a lot of thinking. I realize I've been wrong not to trust you. Your mother and I raised a very intelligent good person, and yet I was afraid of what might happen to you. I'm not afraid any longer. This is not your problem. It's mine. I'm going to go to a professional and get some help for it. I'm willing to go more than halfway to heal our relationship. Would you willing to at least meet me halfway?"

Nicole was quiet for several moments and then she said, "Yes. I can't think of anything I'd rather have than a good relationship with you. I've avoided you more and more during the last two years, and I'm sure that's been part of the problem. We can work on it over the holidays."

He kissed her on the top of her head and then said, "What I don't understand is why Tiffany's here and what this is all about."

"Carl, I can help you with that," Kat said. She told him what she'd found out about Tiffany and why Tiffany had been willing to commit murder to keep her book, The Country Club Cover-Up, from being published. "Now it's my turn, Carl. Why did you come home in the middle of the day? I really didn't expect to see you here at the house."

"You normally wouldn't have, but I wasn't getting anything done at work. I kept thinking about Nancy, and how I was losing Nicole. My boss finally told me to leave. He used the excuse that I should go home because of the storm, but I think the real reason was because he thought I was pretty worthless at work today. I probably shouldn't have gone back to work so soon after Nancy's death, but I wanted something to take my mind off of it."

"Well, I'm glad you got here when you did. Without you, Rudy never would have been able to get in the house." Rudy hadn't moved and his jaws were still clamped around Tiffany's leg. "Rudy, come. You've got to be tired from holding that pose. Tiffany, let me warn you that the dog will attack at my command, so don't try anything. Actually I think I hear a siren and with the streets being empty, I imagine the police chief will be here momentarily."

Kat was right. Minutes later they heard the chief call out, "Kat, where are you?"

"Down the hall in the office."

He strode into the room, his gun in his hand. "Kat, I'll take over. Oh, I brought someone who was with me when you called." Blaine walked into the room and rushed over to Kat.

"Are you all right?" he asked.

"I'm a little shaky, but it's over. Rudy saved our lives. Thank you so much. If you hadn't given him to me, we'd all be dead."

The chief listened as they told him what had happened and how Tiffany had admitted that she was the person who had murdered Nancy. A moment later two of the chief's deputies entered the room. "Take her to jail and book her for murder and attempted murder." He turned to Carl, Nicole, and Kat. "I'm going to need statements from all of you. We can either do it now or you can come to my office tomorrow, however, given the severity of the storm, I'd prefer to do it now. Is that okay with you?"

The three of them agreed they'd rather do it now and get it over with. When he was finally finished taking the statements, he told them they could leave. "Oh, Nicole, one thing more," Kat said. "You told me you'd be driving a little red car. I didn't see one when I pulled in."

"No, I guess the battery went dead from the below freezing temperature. Actually, Lacie drove me here and then left for class. I think I'll stay here tonight. I don't want her to come out here and get me with all this snow."

"Blaine, I can give you a ride back to your office, since you rode here with the chief," Kat said.

"No, I'm going home with you, and I'm driving. You've been through enough today. I'll even make dinner for you. I'm sure I can find something in your well-stocked pantry. Plus, I think Rudy needs to have a special treat. Got any porterhouse or T-bone steaks in your freezer?" he asked, putting her coat on her shoulders. "Let's go. We'll be lucky to get home as it is. I hope you've got snow tires on your car. We're going to need them."

The drive back to Kat's house was difficult, and she was glad Blaine was driving. Night had fallen by the time she'd finished giving her statement to the police chief and the streets were slick and dangerous from the accumulated snow and ice. She breathed a sigh of relief when she, Blaine, and Rudy were safely in her garage.

"The first thing I'm going to do is take a steak out of the freezer, defrost it in the microwave, and give Rudy a well-deserved treat," Kat said. "If it hadn't been for him, I wouldn't be here now. Blaine, I know I've said it before, but I can't thank you enough for giving him to me."

"You don't need to thank me anymore, Kat. I'm just glad you'd taken the time to read the command instructions for Rudy that Casey gave you. What exactly did you do that made Rudy attack Tiffany?"

"The instructions said if you wanted the dog to attack someone and you couldn't give a verbal command, Casey had trained his dogs to obey non-verbal visual commands. It sounds weird, but in this case the person was supposed to pull on their thumb with their opposite hand and point with their index finger in the direction of the person the dog was to attack. The instructions said a hand signal like that wasn't a normal movement, so the dog would understand that it was to attack, but the person who was being attacked wouldn't associate the hand signal with anything abnormal. Like I said, it sounds weird, but it worked."

"Kat, I was with the chief discussing an upcoming case when you called him. I have to tell you my heart was in my throat on the drive from the station to the Jennings' home. I was so afraid something bad had happened to you."

He walked over to her and put his arms around her, gently stroking her hair. "If you'd let me, I'd like to become part of your world. I don't know what it is about you, but now that I've found you, I don't want anything to happen to you."

She lifted her head up and kissed him. "Blaine, it doesn't make any sense to me either, but now that you've come into my world, I don't want to think about what my world would be like without you. You definitely are invited in."

He looked down at her. "Lady, I accept the invitation. Tell you what. While you make the calls you probably need to make, I'll scour the cupboards and refrigerator and come up with something good to eat for dinner. After all, being a bachelor all these years has made me pretty resourceful. I'll take care of the steak and feed the dogs, but I do think Jazz should have a little of the steak before we have to deal with a case of sibling rivalry. Okay with you?"

"Absolutely. Let me go into my office and make some calls, and I'll be back in about an hour."

"Take your time. I'm going to open a bottle of wine and have a glass while I contemplate what gourmet creation I'm going to come up with for dinner. May I bring you one?"

"You sure can. It sounds heavenly after today. While you're at it, why don't you start a fire? I have some firewood in the garage, and there's a box of kindling next to it. You'll also find a stack of newspapers that I recycle near the wood." She turned and walked down the hall to her office to make her calls.

CHAPTER TWENTY-FOUR

An hour later Kat walked into the kitchen and said, "Something smells good, but I can't quite tell what it is. What are you fixing?"

"I'm going to surprise you. You'll have to be patient. How did the calls go?"

"They went well, but before I tell you about them, I want to compliment you on the fire. It's perfect for a stormy cold night."

"Thanks. Comes from being a Boy Scout. Who did you call, and what happened?"

"The first person I called was Barbara. I could tell when I left the club after I talked to her today that she was really concerned. Her husband's out of work, and money is very tight for them. It was quite apparent she was getting near the end of her rope. She was so relieved it was over, and I think she was also relieved that there's no reason for the chief or anyone else to tell the club manager about the part Barbara played in the murder.

"She apologized several times to me. I think it's kind of like a chain reaction. If Barbara hadn't seen the manuscript on the floor, and if she hadn't given it to Tiffany, Nancy would still be alive. I didn't say that to Barbara, but I'm sure it's occurred to her."

"I've always thought she was a very good hostess," Blaine said. "Yes, she's kind of a gossip, but she's warm and friendly, and a country club restaurant needs someone who make the guests feel welcome. Who knows? Maybe she'll think twice about gossiping after this."

"I have no idea. Time will tell. The next person I called was Sally Lonsdale. The police chief told me he'd questioned her when he found out she'd read a copy of my manuscript. I don't know if she realized she might be a suspect, but I called her anyway. I did not get a warm reception, in fact, it was downright chilly. It was very apparent she is not a fan of my books. Oh well, I know they're not for everybody. She said she was glad the murderer had been caught, but she hoped that because of the murder my book wouldn't be published. She told me it was morally wrong to write books like I did, and that at some point, I would be held accountable for my actions. I don't think she and I will ever sing kumbaya together."

"From what I hear, that's no big loss. I rather doubt you'd have enjoyed the experience, anyway. Good riddance," Blaine said.

"The next person I called was your brother. After everything he told me, I thought the murderer must have been Tiffany, but I didn't have a clue how it could be proved. I'm kind of glad it happened the way it did."

"The result was positive, but remember, it also could have been negative."

"I know. I'll just go with what it is. Next I called Lacie. I could tell she was really worried. She has some final exams coming up in the next few days, so I wanted her to be able to direct her full attention towards them. Although she wasn't very thrilled about the danger I'd been in, she was happy the whole thing was over, and the killer had been caught and was now in jail."

"The next person I called was Bev. When I talked to her about editing this morning, she told me how worried she was that if Nancy's death had been about the book, something could happen to me. It's nice to know that people care that much. Finally, I called Carl to let him know we'd all made it home safely and to see how he and Nicole were doing. He told me they were doing very well and were planning Nancy's funeral. He said he hadn't felt right making the plans for Nancy's funeral without Nicole's input. He told me he'd call me when the arrangements were finalized and he'd let me know when the service at the church was going to be held."

"That's about the whole cast of characters, isn't it?" Blaine asked.

"Yes. Now I can put my full attention on the book I'm writing and the one Bev is editing. I think I made a brilliant choice when I asked her to be my editor."

"Why is that?" he asked as he opened the oven door and removed a dish.

"She's already read the manuscript I sent her and has a full page of things she thinks I need to do to make the book better, but here's the interesting part. When I finished telling her what had happened at the Jennings' home, she said, 'That would make a perfect ending for your book.' She's right. Isn't there something about life imitating art? I seem to remember Oscar Wilde writing about it. I suppose my book could loosely be considered art and Tiffany's actions are now going to be the ending of my book, so life and art are pretty much one and the same. What do you think?"

"I think that's really obscure, and no one will get the connection. If you want my advice, I'd say to leave it off the back cover," he said, putting a plate in front of her. "Voila! Dinner is served."

"Blaine, this looks delicious, and it looks like some serious comfort food."

"So it is. It's my version of beef stroganoff, and whenever I've had a bad day at the office, it's my go-to food. Fortunately, you had all the ingredients between the freezer, refrigerator, and pantry. Enjoy!"

A few minutes later she said, "It not only looks delicious, it is. I was really hungry, because I never had lunch. I didn't plan on eating at the club, since all I wanted to do was talk to Barbara, but I thought I could grab a bite on the way to my meeting with Nicole. However, I was running late, and one thing led to another, and you know the rest. Thank you so much for doing this. When we're finished eating, I'll do the dishes, and you can take my car home. I really don't want to drive you home and then drive back here.'

Blaine grinned and said, 'You think I want to go out in this? No way. I'm spending the night. I can sleep in Lacie's room, or maybe..."

She looked over at him and said, "Think it's a little too soon for or maybe..."

RECIPES

EXTRA FUDGY BROWNIES

Ingredients

5 tbsp. unsalted butter, cut into 5 pieces
4 oz. semisweet chocolate, chopped (I use a big knife to chop them. Make sure the cutting board is dry, or you're going to have a big mess on your hands and starting a recipe off with an immediate mess is not fun!)
2 oz. unsweetened chocolate, chopped (Same as above.)
3/4 cup sugar
1/4 tsp. salt
2 large eggs (I use jumbo, but large works well.)
1/3 cup all-purpose flour
1/3 cup walnuts (optional - I don't use them because my grandchildren don't like nuts!)
1/2 cup semisweet chocolate bits

Directions

Preheat oven to 325 degrees. Lightly butter the bottom and sides of a 9 x 13 inch Pyrex glass dish. (Truth be told I bring butter to room temperature and use my fingers, just make sure they're clean.)

Use a double boiler pan and bring the water to a boil in the lower pan. (If you don't have a double boiler you can substitute by putting a glass or metal bowl over a pot of gently simmering water. Slowly heat the butter and the chocolate in the top pan until melted, stirring occasionally. Remove the bowl and whisk in the sugar and salt. When it's cool enough so that the mixture won't cook the eggs, add them, one at a time, stirring to incorporate after each one. Add the flour and mix it in. Gently stir the chocolate bits into the mixture and if desired, the walnuts.

Pour mixture into prepared dish and bake 30 - 35 minutes or until a toothpick inserted in the center comes out clean. Ovens vary so times will too. There are two schools of thought on when a brownie is done. I'm of the just cooked through school, but a lot of people prefer to have them a little drier than I do. Your choice. Cool on a cooking rack and then cut into squares. Enjoy!

BLAINE'S BEEF STROGANOFF

Ingredients

1 lb. sirloin steak
3 tbsp. all-purpose flour
2 tbsp. vegetable oil
1 large onion, finely chopped
8 oz. mushrooms (cut the stem ends off and quarter them)
2 tbsp. chili sauce
1 tsp. salt
1/4 tsp pepper
1 cup sour cream
1 16 oz. pkg. wide butter noodles
2 tbsp. chopped chives for garnish

Directions

Put the steak on a cutting board and cut it into approximately 1 inch square pieces. Put the flour in a paper or plastic bag and add one-fourth of the beef pieces. Shake the bag so the pieces become coated. Meanwhile, heat the oil in a large deep pan over medium heat. When it's hot remove the pieces from the bag and brown them in the oil, about 2 minutes on each side. When both sides have been browned, remove them and set aside. Repeat with 1/4 of the pieces at a time. When the last batch has been removed from the oil, add the chopped onion and sauté until soft. Return the meat to the pan and add the chili sauce, salt, and pepper. Cover and simmer for approximately one hour or until the meat is tender.

When the meat is tender bring the water for the noodles to a boil and prepare them according to the directions on the package.

Just before serving stir one cup of the meat mixture into the sour cream and then return that mixture to the remaining meat mixture, stirring to combine. (I know it sounds like an unnecessary step, but trust me on this one) Heat slowly until the entire mixture is warm. Drain the noodles. Put a serving of noodles in a soup bowl or spaghetti bowl. Top with the meat mixture and garnish with the chives. Enjoy!

NOTE: You can also serve this over rice or mashed potatoes.

COMFORT FOOD LINGUINI WITH CLAM SAUCE

Ingredients

1 box linguini
1 tbsp. olive oil
½ cup diced onions
3 cloves garlic, minced
2 (10 oz.) cans whole baby clams, drained (I used minced and chopped for years, but I found that whole clams really make a difference)
1 tsp. dried oregano
8 oz. bottle clam juice
½ cup chicken broth (If I don't have homemade broth on hand, I prefer the concentrated brand that comes in a jar called 'Better

than Bouillon' to cubes)
½ cup dry white wine
Salt and pepper
¼ cup chopped fresh parsley

Directions

Bring a large pot of water to a boil and add enough salt so that it tastes like the ocean. Cook the linguini according to the directions on the package. You want the linguini to just be done, not mushy.

While you're bringing the water to a boil, heat the oil in a large skillet over medium heat. Add the diced onions and sauté until tender. When tender, add the garlic and cook for about a minute. Add the clams and sauté 2 more minutes. Add the oregano, salt, pepper and gently combine. Finally, add the clam juice, chicken broth, and wine and bring the mixture to a boil. Reduce the heat and simmer 5 minutes. Pour the clam mixture over the drained linguine. You can add the parsley and stir to combine or use it along with the Parmesan as a garnish. I like to serve it in pasta bowls. Enjoy!

CHICKEN MANICOTTI WITH ITALIAN SAUSAGE

Ingredients

1 box of manicotti noodles
1 jar of marinara sauce
1 tbsp. olive oil
2 cloves of garlic, finely chopped
1 onion, finely chopped
2 skinless chicken breasts or thighs (It's usually cheaper if you buy them with the skin on and then remove it)
3 Italian sausages with the casings removed, torn into small bite size pieces
¼ tsp salt
¼ tsp pepper

1 tsp. Italian seasoning
1 pint ricotta cheese
½ cup shredded mozzarella cheese
Optional: Fresh parsley leaves, minced

Directions

Preheat the oven to 350 degrees. Put the skinless chicken in an ovenproof pan and bake, covered with tin foil, for 45 minutes. Let cool. When cool, shred or cut into bite-size pieces and set aside. Fry the sausage pieces over medium heat and set aside.

Bring a large pot of water to a boil. Add the salt until it tastes like the ocean. Cook the manicotti according to the package instructions. Drain and immediately transfer the manicotti noodles to a large bowl of ice water with plenty of ice cubes.

While you're cooking the manicotti noodles, put the olive oil in a small frying pan. Heat the oil over medium heat. When hot, add the chopped onion and sauté until soft. Add the garlic and cook for 1 more minute. Remove and set aside.

Combine the ricotta cheese, chicken, sausage, egg, Italian seasoning, sautéed onions, garlic, ¼ tsp salt, and ¼ tsp. pepper in a mixing bowl.

If you have oval individual dishes, spread ¼ cup of the marinara sauce in each one. If not, spread one cup of the marinara in a 9 x 13" pan. Gently remove the cooked manicotti noodles, one at a time, from the ice water and stuff them with the cheese, chicken, and sausage mixture. (It's messy, and I've found the best way to do it is with my hands. Not particularly fun, but it works! Some of the noodles will probably tear. Don't worry about it, just put the torn side down and no one but you will ever know.) If you're using individual dishes, put two stuffed manicotti noodles in each dish. If you're using the large pan, fill the noodles, allowing about ½ inch between them. Spoon the remaining marinara sauce over the noodles and place them side by side in a pan. Sprinkle 2 tablespoons of the shredded mozzarella cheese on top of each of the individual dishes.

If using one large dish, sprinkle all of the mozzarella cheese on it and the remaining marinara sauce. Bake at 350 for 40 minutes. I like to sprinkle a little parsley on the top just before serving. Enjoy!

KAT'S COFFEE CAKE

Ingredients for Coffee Cake

2 cups Bisquick mix
2/3 cup milk
2 tbs. granulated sugar
1 egg

Ingredients for Streusel Swirl:

½ cup Bisquick mix
½ cup brown sugar
½ tsp. ground cinnamon
3 tbsp. firm butter cut into 12 pieces
Optional: ½ cup walnuts or pecans (Like I said earlier, my grandchildren are not fans of nuts)

Directions

Preheat oven to 375 degrees. Lightly oil a 9" round baking dish. In a medium bowl, prepare the coffee cake by combining the Bisquick mix, milk, sugar and the egg. Spread the mixture in the prepared pan. In a small bowl prepare the streusel by combining the Bisquick mix, brown sugar, cinnamon, and butter. Spoon it over the coffee cake. Using a table knife, push it back and forth through the streusel mixture so as to swirl the streusel into the coffee cake mixture. If desired, top with the nuts. Bake 20 – 25 minutes or until brown on top. Enjoy!

Amazing Ebooks & Paperbacks for FREE

Go to www.dianneharman.com/freepaperback.html and get your FREE copies of Dianne's books and Dianne's favorite recipes immediately by signing up for her newsletter.

Once you've signed up for her newsletter you're eligible to win autographed paperbacks. One lucky winner is picked every week. Hurry before the offer ends.

ABOUT THE AUTHOR

Dianne lives in Huntington Beach, California, with her husband, Tom, a former California State Senator, and her boxer dog, Kelly. Her passions are cooking, reading, and dogs, so whenever she has a little free time, you can either find her in the kitchen, playing with Kelly in the back yard, or curled up with the latest book she's reading.

Her award winning books include:

Cedar Bay Cozy Mystery Series
Kelly's Koffee Shop, Murder at Jade Cove, White Cloud Retreat, Marriage and Murder, Murder in the Pearl District, Murder in Calico Gold, Murder at the Cooking School, Murder in Cuba, Trouble at the Kennel

Liz Lucas Cozy Mystery Series
Murder in Cottage #6, Murder & Brandy Boy, The Death Card, Murder at The Bed & Breakfast, The Blue Butterfly

High Desert Cozy Mystery Series
Murder & The Monkey Band, Murder & The Secret Cave

Midwest Cozy Mystery Series
Murdered by Words

Coyote Series
Blue Coyote Motel, Coyote in Provence, Cornered Coyote

Website: www.dianneharman.com
Blog: www.dianneharman.com/blog
Email: dianne@dianneharman.com

Newsletter
If you would like to be notified of her latest releases please go to www.dianneharman.com and sign up for her newsletter.

Made in the USA
Middletown, DE
23 July 2016